Advance Praise For
BIG GIANT FLOATING HEAD

"One afternoon I was staring at the page when I heard a fluttering at the window. I looked up and saw a story beating its wings against the glass." —Frog or Foil

"For years I've been hoping someone would write about the relationship between _____ and Christopher Boucher. And now someone finally has! I just wish it could have been someone else." —Television Smith

"Solitude is the art form of the twenty-first century."
—Carney

"It was a story about my mother." —*Bad Sandwich*

"I opened the window and tried to coax the story out, but then ▉ came in and started swatting at the thing. 'What are you doing?' I said." —Calorie Thompson

"I really consider the short story an inferior form."
—*Lipolou Today*

"I mean, I read as many of these things as I could. But they're all just so depressing!" —The Memory of Richard

"But before I could stop her, she hit the story with a shoe and it fell to the ground." —*The Daily Wheel*

"I wouldn't stay at the Tetherly again if you paid me a million dollars." —Grayson

"Wait—I thought that story died a long time ago." —*Graveyard Monthly*

"'Look what you did,' I said, picking up the dead story. 'This house is infested! I can't take it anymore!'" —She Said.

"But the story wasn't yet dead. I could feel its heart beating, see its wings fluttering. It opened its eyes and looked me right in the face." —Resin

"And now the story was *furious*." —*New Candide*

BIG GIANT FLOATING HEAD

CHRISTOPHER BOUCHER

MELVILLE HOUSE
BROOKLYN • LONDON

BIG GIANT FLOATING HEAD

Melville House Publishing
46 John Street
Brooklyn, NY 11201
and
Melville House UK
Suite 2000
16/18 Woodford Road
London E7 0HA

mhpbooks.com
@melvillehouse

Grateful acknowledgment is made to the editors of the
publications in which portions of this book first appeared, in
slightly different form: *The 2018 Short Story Advent Calendar*,
Columbia Journal, *Conjunctions Online*, *Cutthroat*, *draft: The Journal
of Process*, *Electric Literature*, and *Keyhole Magazine*.

ISBN: 978-1-61219-757-9
ISBN: 978-1-61219-758-6 (eBook)

Designed by Betty Lew

Printed in the United States of America

10 9 8 7 6 5 4 3 2 1

A catalog record is available for this book from the Library of
Congress

THE FLOATING HEADS

BIG
GIANT
FLOATING
HEAD

BIG GIANT FLOATING HEAD

I first saw the Big Giant Floating Head on the same day that my wife Liz announced on Twitter that she didn't love me any-more. You can go back on her timeline and read the tweet: *@bouchergutter, I don't love you anymore. Not sure I ever did!* Then she tweeted out a picture of the letter I'd sent her three days earlier, in which I apologized and asked for forgiveness, along with the caption, *Cant wait to finally DIVORCE this loser.*

I didn't see Liz's tweet at first because I was riding my bike through town, a twelve-foot aluminum gutter drain balanced on my shoulder. I wasn't particularly good at gutterwork, but I hadn't completely failed at it yet either—not like I had at marriage, and writing, and most everything else. For years before that I'd worked in fiction—as a novelist, bookseller, editor, verb salesman, you name it. But I'd hurt people—hurt *myself*—with my last book, a novel called *Golden Delicious*. That story's too sad for me to tell, suffice it to say that someone died because of me and I subsequently gave up writing and books altogether. Something broke inside me when I did, though: A heart-sized hole formed in my chest; my imagination grew a beard and its spine began to curve. Then I began drinking, lost my driver's license, and got kicked out of my own house. Not even the bike was mine—I was borrowing it from Bill Sunflower, a gutter guy I worked with who was letting me crash at his place while things cooled down with my wife. Liz and I had gone through this kind of thing before, but every time she took me back. When I checked my phone at the corner of Main and Lex that day, though, I saw her tweet and my stomach roiled. There was a thought in my head, a literal voice, that said, *It's over, Chris. Like,* over-*over.*

I changed course and pedaled home—it was only a few blocks away. Liz was working from home at the time, and she was sitting at the kitchen table and saw me approaching. She stood up and grabbed her phone, threw open the window, and started shouting at me. You can see it all on her timeline: me standing in the driveway next to my own pickup truck (which I wasn't allowed to drive at the time), the bike and the drain at my feet, shouting awful things at Liz. And look how beautiful she is—her fireplace eyes, her hair a parade—even as she shouts back at me, "You're drunk!"

"No I *ain't!*" I say, though I clearly am.

Then you can hear the wrinkle of paper: Liz's holding my letter. "You were drunk when you wrote *this*, too!"

"No, sir!" I say.

"Oh, really?" Liz holds the letter in front of the phone. "I'm not a man of worlds," she says. "What's a man of worlds?"

"Words, I meant!" I say.

"I know I've mistake," she continues. "You've mistaked?"

Then you can hear me say, "Liz."

"Do you *mistake* often, Chris?"

"Liz," I say again, my voice as thin as paper. "What is *that*?"

Then Liz says "Holy—," and the phone turns off.

"—shit," is what Liz said next, when she saw what I was pointing at. "Is that a—"

"It's an eye," I said. It was: a giant eye, staring at me through the trees behind the Camerlenghis' house. "There's another one next to it," I said. I crossed the street. "It's a *face!*" I shouted. From that angle I could see the whole thing: blue eyes, brown hair, chin stubble—a big giant floating head, staring right at me with a smile on his face like he was listening to a joke.

Liz came outside. "Jesus Christ, Chris," she said.

Then Glen Camerlenghi swung open his porch door. "Leo won't stop barking," he said. He looked up and saw the face. "What the hey is that?"

I crossed back to our side of the street.

"It's moving—Chris, it's moving!" Liz said. "It's following you!"

It was. I took a few strides down the sidewalk and the Big Giant Floating Head moved with me. "Crap," I said.

"It's some sort of fancy drone," said Glen. "Right?"

I ran back across the street and picked up my bike.

"Chris?" said Liz.

"I'm calling the police," said Glen.

I hoisted the drain over my shoulder and mounted the bike.

"Where are you going?" Liz shouted at me.

I started pedaling and the Big Giant Floating Head followed. I sped up and the head sped up too. I took a sharp turn on Gore and the face stayed with me—hopping trees, lifting over buildings, dropping lower in clearings. There was no outrunning it. Two or three people shouted at me along the way—"Hey!" one said; "Look up!" said another—and at the light on Argyle an old man in a blue van kept beeping at me. I stopped at the crosswalk and gave him the finger, and he rolled down his window. "There's a big giant head above you, guy!"

"No shit!" I said. Then I saw a gap in the crossing traffic and pedaled away from him.

Two blocks from Bill's house, though, I heard a police siren and I saw blue flashing lights behind me. I looked back: it was Cass Donner, who used to stop me all the time when I was driving and had once arrested me for public drunkenness. Cass was OK—not as bad as some of the other cops in town. I stopped pedaling and she got out of the cruiser and stared up at the face. "What do you know about this, Boucher?" she said.

I shook my head. "Picked it up at my house, followed me here."

"It's *following* you?"

"Seems to stay just that far behind me," I said.

The face smiled down at Cass.

Cass took a photo of the face with her phone. "Just stay there, OK?" she said, and she ducked into her cruiser, where I heard her say something into her walkie.

I put down the gutter and checked my phone. There was a text from Liz: *Where r u is that thing still followng u?*

I didn't reply. There was another one from Bill. *Waitin on that drain*, he wrote.

Got held up, I replied. *Be there in a few.*

Then Cass appeared behind me. "I want you to just hang tight for a few minutes, OK?"

I got off my bike.

Cass looked down at the drain. "Gutter drain?"

"Yuh-huh," I said.

"For your place?"

I shook my head. "Working with Bill Sunflower."

"Holy moly—*that* guy," she said.

Then a fire truck pulled up in front of me and two guys hopped down from the cab. One was Al McLeod, who was in the class behind me at Coolidge High; the other guy I didn't know.

"Like I told you," said Cass to the second guy.

McLeod put his hand over his eyes, as if blocking out the sun. "Just hanging there like that?"

"Following our friend Christopher here," said Cass.

McLeod found his phone and took a picture of the face.

"Let's get up there," said the other guy, and McLeod nodded. They got back in the truck, moved it thirty or so yards down the road, and parked under the face. Then McLeod raised a ladder off the back of the truck and the other guy climbed it. When he reached the top of the ladder he was about twenty feet below the Big Giant Floating Head. "Whoa," he said.

"What is it?" shouted McLeod.

"It's breathing!" shouted the guy.

Al looked back at Cass and me.

The firefighter scrambled down the ladder. "Fucking thing is breathing," he said.

Cass and McLeod met him on the ground and they huddled and talked about what to do.

What the fuck C, texted Bill.

I sat down on the curb. *Cops here*, I typed. *Waiting for them to let me go.*

By this point, some neighbors were gathering on the sidewalk. Then another cop car pulled up and a cop I didn't know got out and ran over to Cass.

WHAT, Bill texted. *Wht did u do?*

Nothing, explain it when I get there.

Finally, Cass walked over to me and I stood up to talk to her. "Well," she said. "We're going to get the word out and see what we can find out. In the meantime, we'll just keep an eye on it."

I nodded.

"You think it'll keep following you?"

"Guess we'll see," I said.

Cass signaled to the cops and the firefighters and they all got into their vehicles. Then I picked up the bike, threw my leg over the bar, and started pedaling. Sure enough, the face moved right alongside me, smiling all the while, a procession of vehicles with flashing lights trailing behind it. We took a left on Dale and a right on Outlaw; Bill's house was a block down on the right. Bill was drinking a beer on the porch—"meditating," as he called it—but he stood up when he saw the whole procession: me, the face, the cruisers and fire truck parking at the curb. I dropped the gutter in the grass and walked up the steps. "What the *fuck*," he said, looking at the face.

"I told you," I said.

"What is that—some sort of balloon?"

I shrugged. "It's been following me all through town."

Bill seemed to be trying to form a question, but before he could, a white van with the News 23 insignia pulled up behind the fire truck. Bill went inside; I followed, and found him standing near the fridge. "I don't like cops," he said, "and I don't like cameras."

"What do you expect, there's a fucking face in the sky," I said.

He shook his head. "Face or no face," he said.

When I went back outside, a reporter was interviewing the neighbors. Eventually he approached me. "Is it true that you found the face?" he asked, holding a microphone out to me.

"More like it found me," I said.

"Were you frightened?"

"At first, yeah—I saw these two eyes staring at me through the trees." I looked back at the face. "But he seems pretty friendly."

Soon it got dark, and the neighbors started going inside. Then I did, too. Bill was sitting on the couch, looking through the curtains, the lights of the fire truck shining off his bald head. I sat down and said, "You should see what Liz posted about me."

"I saw it," he said. "That's rough, bud."

"Think she means it?"

"Who knows," Bill said.

I sipped my beer and moved the curtain aside. The face hung there, smiling like a dumbass.

Bill finished his beer and went to bed. I stayed up for another few minutes, watching the face, and then I turned off the lights and fell asleep on the couch. I slept for maybe an hour, during which I dreamt of a supermarket. Only, I could see the building from above—see the tops of peoples' heads, the roofs of cars in the parking lot, a bird perched on a ledge near a steam vent.

When I woke up again, the street was dark. I didn't see the cops, or the news, or the face. As I was watching, though, I saw a flicker in the sky and the face reappeared, just where it had been.

I lay back down. When I opened my eyes, Bill was standing over me and holding my boots. "What time is it?" I said.

"Five," he said.

I sat up and took my boots.

"Face still there?"

Bill nodded. "But don't worry, I know what to do."

I looked through the curtain. The face smiled at me.

"Let's move," said Bill.

Bill grabbed a rolled-up wool blanket from the ottoman and walked out into the dark morning. He shoved the blanket behind the seat, started up the engine and took a left on Highland. Then he looked in the rearview and said, "That fucker following us?"

"Yup," I said.

"Good," said Bill. "Keep an eye out for cops." Right on Hawthorne. "Still following?"

"Yuh-huh." The Big Giant Floating Head hung high in the back window—I watched it drift over trees and buildings, its face still mildly amused, as if it were saying, *Where to next, buddy?*

Bill drove another mile and then pulled over next to Corso Field, which was empty except for two joggers running laps. With the face about a hundred yards away and floating toward us, Bill kicked open his door, reached behind the seat and pulled out a shotgun. "Bill," I said.

"Shh," he said. He leaned the shotgun against the top of the cab and waited for the face to get closer. "Keep smiling, mofo," he said.

"You don't have to do this," I said.

Bill fired. The joggers stopped and turned to us, but the face didn't seem to notice. Bill fired the gun again. Then the face frowned and started falling. "Let's get it," he said. He drove the truck out onto the field. By the time we got there, the joggers were standing over the deflated face. "Get out of there!" Bill boomed at them, and they backed up.

"Is that a kite?" said one of the joggers.

"Yeah, it's a kite," said Bill.

"No it isn't," said the other. "That thing was on the news last night."

Bill and I leaned over the face. It was bleeding in the forehead. "Christ," Bill said. "It's a real fucking face." It was: real hair and skin; two giant eyes; nostrils the size of manholes. It folded over itself like a parachute. Suddenly I felt sick to my stomach; I stumbled over to the treeline and puked.

"Bowcher!" Bill shouted, and I could tell from his tone that he was disgusted with me. "Let's get this thing out of here."

I ran back across the field and we started rolling up the face. It was heavy and still warm. We hoisted it onto the back of the truck. The joggers shouted something, but we jumped into the truck, coughed the engine on, and drove across the field and back onto the road.

"What the *fuck*," I said. I wished we'd brought some beer.

"Hey, I stopped asking questions a long time ago," said Bill.

"You can't bring it back to your place," I said. "Cops'll know."

Bill took a right on Highland.

"Bill," I said.

"It's taken care of, OK?"

I shut up and sat back in my seat. We crossed the West Brix line, turned off of Main and onto Haskell, and then drove a long way out, until I wasn't even sure which town we were in. Then we passed some barbed-wire fence and Bill turned into the parking lot of a storage facility. He parked outside one of the garage bays and opened the door. "Let's do this quick," he said. He pulled up the garage door and gestured for me to help him lift the face. I took hold of one of the ears; the face was cold now, and starting to stiffen. Bill didn't say anything as we hauled the carcass into the dark, damp storage unit. We put the face down on the cement while Bill cleared a space, and I straightened up and looked around. I saw some old furniture, a bunch of half-crushed cardboard boxes, at least thirty black plastic bags. I didn't ask what all this was. Bill'd taken his share of hits over the years: he'd been married, had a son who died of cancer. He didn't talk about these things.

"Here," Bill said. "Move it here." We stuffed the face and the gun behind a treadmill and a foam-core picture of Bill at least thirty pounds lighter. He had all his hair and he was standing next to a woman with a mullet and a Hartford Whalers sweatshirt. I'd seen pictures of his ex-wife—this wasn't her. "Who's that?" I said.

"No one," said Bill. "That's no one." Then he ushered me out of the storage unit, pulled the door down to the ground, and locked the latch.

When we got back to Bill's, the news van and a police car were parked outside. A different cop, an old man I didn't recognize, got out of his cruiser and approached our truck. "Where is it?" he said.

"Where is what?" Bill said.

"The *face*," said the cop.

Bill shrugged.

"It left late last night," I said, "flew off somewhere."

Then a guy spilled out of the news van and hustled over. "Where'd it go?"

"We've got reports saying it was around here this morning," said the cop.

"That's a relief," I said. "We were just out looking for him."

The cop turned to Bill. "How about you, Sunflower?"

"How 'bout me what?" said Bill.

"Where is the face?" said the news reporter.

The cop said, "Did you do something here?"

"Like what?" said Bill.

"Let me get in your house," said the cop.

"Sure," said Bill. "Got a warrant?"

The cops and the news stayed for a few more minutes, and cruisers circled past Bill's house every few hours over the next few days. Liz texted repeatedly to ask what happened to the face, but I stopped replying. Four days after its disappearance, Joyce O'Lar from News 9 interviewed me and said a police report had been filed about the gunfire. "Oh no," I said, feigning shock. "Was anyone injured?"

"But you didn't see the face that morning," said O'Lar.

I tried to make my face look pained. "Last I saw it was Thursday night. Then it just floated away."

Soon the Big Giant Floating Head was forgotten. And I don't know what happened to the carcass in the storage unit—whether Bill disposed of it, or it rotted in there or disintegrated. Bill and I never talked about it. Mostly we talked about gutters. It was October, and we had a lot of jobs lined up: three installations, four repairs, at least twenty cleanings. Everyone wanted us to get there before the snow fell, and we worked our asses off to keep up.

Then, that Friday, two days before Halloween, I got my driver's license reinstated. Soon as I did, I rode my bike over to my house—Liz's house, our house, whatever—to get my truck. I expected to see it in the driveway as usual, but it wasn't there. So I dropped my bike in the yard and knocked on the door. Liz answered, holding a big hardcover library book under her arm. "The villain returns," she said.

Despite our arguments, our break-ups, the time she cheated on me, even, I loved Liz; I'd loved her since the moment I first saw her strumming her guitar at the open mic at Café Attitude six years earlier. It's true that I wrote that letter on the back of an outstanding utility bill. But it had been so long since I'd tried to express myself on the page. And I'd once thought of myself as a writer! That seemed like a lifetime ago now. I said some things in that letter, though, that I hoped would mean something to her—that I thought might change things between us. *This DUI has really woken me up*, I wrote. *I understand everything now.* Though I guess I had misspelled "everything." *I still have all these stories in my head that I want to get out on paper. And I'm going to do it, swear to God.*

"Just here to get my truck," I said.

"Wait, wait," she said. She held up her phone. "The villain returns," she repeated. "Say hello, villain."

"Where is it?" I said.

Liz turned the camera on herself. "Watch this," she said, and then turned the phone back on me.

"Come on, I'm late," I said.

"I sold it," she said.

"Sold what?" I said, dumbly. And then, "You're kidding."

"No—I'm not," she said.

That truck had been Liz's wedding present to me. "Liz," I said. "You didn't."

"Aw. Don't cry, villain," she said.

I was so shocked I couldn't speak. "You—," I began, and then, "How—" And then I said, "Everything in that letter was true."

"None of it was ever true." That's really what she said—you can see it on Facebook. And that may sound harsh, but she had every right to talk to me that way—for years I'd been an asshole to her. Plus, Liz was dating a lot of other people by then. She'd post their dates, or snippets of them, on YouTube. There was one guy who was a magician—he was really handsome. Maybe he was the one telling her to be so tough on me. Or maybe it was someone else—I don't know.

"I miss living here," I said.

"Say goodbye, villain," said Liz.

I walked outside, picked up the bike, and pedaled away.

I wasn't really late for anything—that part had been a lie. Truth was, I wasn't going to work at all—I was meeting Bill and a few other lugs we worked with—Addie Trawl, Gil Murphy, Tall John—at the Black Cat to celebrate getting my license back. I walked into the bar and Bill held up a full bottle of beer. "Alright!" he said. "First round's on me!"

I shook my head and climbed onto a stool.

"What's the problem?" said Bill.

"She sold it," I said.

"The truck?"

"Liz *sold* it," I said.

"Holy shit." He handed me a beer, and we were quiet for a minute. Then he said, "How'd she even have the title?"

"Engagement present," I said.

"*Fuck.*" He sipped his beer. "Well, you'll figure something out. Or *we* will. OK?"

I shrugged. "I loved that truck," I said.

"Drink your beer," Bill said.

I drank that beer and then another. Halfway through my third, Bill elbowed me. "You know who the real loser is here, is me. Cuz I have to keep dragging your sorry ass all over town."

"You love it," I said.

"Like hell," he said.

Then we did some shots, and Gum was there, along with Fay and the Sorry twins. We watched some of the game on TV, and the room got warm and dark. "Man," I said at one point to someone. "I need my *wheels*, man. I need *wheels*."

"Stop saying that," Gum said.

"Stop saying *what*?"

"Just stop it, man," said Gum. Then things got foggy, and I remember Bill putting a hand on my shoulder and saying something about tomorrow, tomorrow, and then Tall John saying, "Whoa! Will you fucking look at that?" and showing Bill his phone, and Bill grabbing the phone and handing it over to me. The screen held a picture of my face—bald head, patchy beard, red nose and all—only detached from my body and floating over a skyscraper. "What," I said, pointing, "what—what—"

"That's Bowcher, right?" said Tall John.

It wasn't just *my* face—there were ten or so other giant floating faces in the frame.

"Is that real?" I said.

And then that same image—the Big Giant Floating Heads floating over the skyscraper—appeared on TV, before switching to footage of giant faces elsewhere: some over the ocean; two over a gravel pit; a gaggle of faces over a soccer match, the players below looking dumbfounded. Some of the faces were moving—following people—and others were floating still. They were faces of all type and origin. Some had long shadowy hair and some were completely bald. Some were gaunt, and some had jowls, and some were very old. But they all had that same smile as the face we shot.

The news showed my face on TV again and Tall John said, "Says that building is in Japan." Meanwhile, my phone was going crazy with messages and tweets. Liz tagged me in a tweet about the skyscraper. *That's my husband!* said the caption.

I put a hand on Bill's shoulder. "I need to get out of here," I said. He led me outside and put me in his truck.

"You OK to drive?" I asked him.

Bill slapped himself in the face. "Yup," he said. He slapped himself again. "I'm fine." Then he started up the engine and pulled out of the lot. I checked my phone again. "They're all over the place, Bill. Some people are calling them clouds."

"Those aren't fucking clouds," said Bill, turning onto Kemp.

"That building's in Tokyo," I said. "Why is my face in Tokyo?"

"Hey. Personally?" he said. "I think it's kind of cool."

"It ain't your face," I said.

"I know it's not." He burped. "But maybe mine's out there too."

By the end of the week there were hundreds of faces in the sky, then thousands, then millions. That winter, everything was faces—they were all anyone could talk about. The late night talk shows had a field day, and all the news outlets interviewed experts in meteorology and astrology. The floating heads made some people nervous—there were reports of more shootings before an international committee made it illegal—but most people embraced them. By early December you could buy bobbleheads of giant faces, artsy posters of faces at sunrise or sunset. Plus, people set up cameras all over the world to track the faces—there were dozens of sites online to identify them and match them to their lookalikes. I'd check the webcams every day to see how my face was doing. He'd drifted away from the skyscraper and over Tokyo Bay, and then he was spotted in a city called Chiba. Since then he'd held steady.

And I don't know about you—assuming you saw your face up there, which most people did—but having that smiling face in the sky changed me. Those weeks before the faces appeared I was pretty down in the dumps. Most afternoons, I'd sit on Bill's porch after work and just drink and stare at my phone. Sometimes I'd open Google Maps and search for my own house—the one I wasn't welcome in anymore. The app would show me a picture of it and directions from here to there. I don't know when that picture was taken, but it looked to be sometime the previous summer—the leaves are still on the trees and our garden hose is coiled up on the lawn. Both cars are in the driveway, too, which means we both might be home. Sitting there on

Bill's porch, I'd zoom in on my living room window, looking for a shape or a shadow. Is Liz in there? Am I?

The floating heads brought me some sort of clarity, though. Soon after their arrival, I stopped drinking so much. I became more thoughtful, more optimistic. I guess I started to think that, if my Skyface was smiling, maybe he knew something I didn't. About my outcome. About how everything would turn out. His face told me everything would be OK, and maybe it would.

And then, that January, a wonderful thing happened when a face that looked like Liz's—not *her*, exactly, but close (sort of close, if I'm being honest)—appeared floating over the Sagamanadi Sea. Over a period of two weeks, Liz's face drifted closer and closer to my face, until the two faces were in the same city, the same neighborhood. Liz saw this and texted me a screenshot with the message, *HOLY SHIT.* There we were—or our faces, or our sort-of faces—floating next to each other in the sky. I didn't text back, but the next day—a Sunday—I was sitting on Bill's porch when Liz pulled up in my truck, got out, and stood beside it.

"My truck," I said.

"Hi, Liz," said Bill.

"Have you seen our faces?" she said.

"You said you sold it," I said.

"I let my brother use it for a while," she said, and her smile was a lot like the smile on her Skyface. "Have you seen them?"

I nodded.

"Come on," she said.

"Just like that?"

"What do you want, flowers?" she said. "Want me to beg?"

"No," I said.

"Tell you what." She walked around to the passenger seat door. "You can drive," she said. Then she got in and closed the door.

I stood up, walked down to the truck, got, in and drove us home.

·✦·

I won't lie to you: those first few weeks after I moved back in with Liz weren't easy—we still argued, stormed out on each other, and threatened to never come back. But our faces really helped us. Whenever things got super tough, we'd turn on facefeed.com and look in on our faces—SkyChris and SkyLiz, that's what we called them—and that would calm us down and give us some perspective. Seeing my face reminded me that there was happiness *somewhere*—even in the darkest moments, when you didn't know how you were going to get along, you could look up at the sky and see something smiling at you: the stars. The moon. A tree. The pattern in a sidewalk tile. The shape your shoelace makes. A giant floating head.

And sometimes it was almost like we heard their voices. *Give yourself a break*, they seemed to say to us, or, *Be nice to each other*. And we tried. Like, if Liz had a gripe, I'd just listen to her and wouldn't talk at all. Even if she said something that pissed me off—about her having feelings for our neighbor Glen, or how sometimes she just wanted a quiet house with no one in it, not me or anyone else—I just: listened. Because that's what she needed most. And I think that's what my face would have wanted.

In my mind, too, something was opening up. I started having new ideas for stories: a guy grows a wall in his mind; he takes a job praying; he competes in a failure competition; he sees big giant floating heads in the sky. And I know these ideas had something to do with SkyChris. Just his being there, watching me from above, was invigorating. It was like he was *reading* me, seeing me move across the page. Or was I seeing *myself*?

I wasn't the only one who changed, either. For a short time there, it seemed like the whole world quieted down a little. There was a temporary cease-fire in Afghanistan, for example, and a new peace treaty between Israel and Palestine. Locally, tensions eased between Coolidge and Blix. It was like we all became more self-aware—like we became better listeners.

Soon, Liz and I started planning a trip to Japan to see our faces in person. This was pretty common—a lot of people were organizing "face quests," including Bill, who went to Scotland in May and left me all his clients. For a long time afterward people asked me about him. "I haven't seen him," I told them, which was true—I don't know what happened to him.

With more jobs than I could handle on my own, though, Liz started working with me. She was good at gutters—meticulous, patient—and we made pretty good money, enough to put a little away each month. Plus, we seemed to get along better when we worked together; for the first time, we were true partners. When I think back on that summer, I remember working on the gutters at the old brush factory, Liz on one ladder and me on another, a motherly face who we nicknamed Maude floating in the horse fields behind that building.

That July, I wrote my first story in two years. It was *this* story, the story of the Big Giant Floating Heads. I let Liz read it, and she said, "Yeah."

"Yeah?" I said.

"It's quirky," she said. "I think it could be part of something longer. A whole novel, maybe."

I bristled. "A novel? I don't know."

"Why not? Because of the last one? That was years ago now," she said. "You're not going to hurt anyone like that again. And besides, I want to know what happens to this guy."

I looked down at the Christopher Boucher on the page. He looked back up at me.

"Hey," said my wife, playfully crashing her shoulder into mine. "Am I supposed to be Liz?"

I smirked. "Yes and no."

"Because she's kind of a bitch," Liz said.

I shrugged. "It's like you said—it's just a better story that way."

One day that August, Liz tweeted: *I love @bouchergutter so much.* Just out of the blue—just to be nice. Which was maybe one of the best things to ever happen to me. I printed out that tweet and put it on the fridge.

By the end of the summer, we'd saved up enough to fly to Chiba. We bought tickets and made the arrangements. Two days before our flight, though, I came home to find Liz crunched up in the corner of the couch. "What's wrong?" I said.

She held out her phone. It showed a face floating over a silo, but the face was frowning. *L@@k at this,* said the tweet. *What's the matter Mr. Face?*

"Where is this?" I said.

"Somewhere in Georgia."

"Sheesh," I said. I didn't think much of it, but Liz was obsessed with it. That night we went to see my brother's jazz band at a sketchy café in East Coolidge, and Liz spent the whole time looking at her phone. She kept holding it out to me and showing me pictures of frowning faces: webcams had picked them up in Reykjavík, Las Vegas, Mexico City, Tarry, Galway, all over.

When we got back home, I turned on the news. CNN had on a special analyst who studied these faces for a living. "Let's not forget," said the expert, "these entities are pretty new."

"The faces, you mean," said the host.

"It's possible they have happy seasons and sad seasons."

"Why a sad season, Dr. Orf?" said the host.

The analyst shrugged. "For the same reason *we* have sad seasons, Maura."

"Maybe they're unhappy for a specific reason."

Orf placed his hands on the desk. "Maybe we've done something wrong."

Liz rubbed her face with her hands. "Should we still go?" she said.

"Go where?"

"To Japan," she said.

"What do you mean? Absolutely we should," I said.

And we did—about a month after The Frowning began, we flew the seventeen hours to Tokyo. That might sound like a long time to be in the air, but it was nice—we shut off our phones and just talked. We played Cards Against Humanity. We watched a movie. "Do you know what?" Liz said about halfway through the movie.

I took off my headphones and looked at her.

"I've never been happier. Not in my whole fucking life."

"Me neither," I said.

When we landed, though, we turned on our phones and saw breaking news about the faces: while we were in the air, some faces had started growling at each other, bumping up against one another, even pushing each other across the sky. We watched it all as a car drove us through downtown Tokyo—waves of people rushing along sidewalks that ran past eloquent, twisty skyscrapers—and toward Chiba. At one point, Liz put her hand on my arm and said, "Chris, look." Then she pointed into the sky, at one floating head scowling at another.

Soon we were out of Tokyo, and driving down a country road through farmlands towards Chiba. Liz had a translation app on her phone, and we used it to tell the driver the exact address of our faces. I'd suggested we check into our hotel first, but Liz said she couldn't wait another minute to see SkyLiz and SkyChris. Suddenly, the driver turned a corner and there they were: my big giant floating face—or, sort of my face; I had more hair, didn't I?—next to a face that, now that I saw it up close, barely looked like Liz at all. Still, it was a stunning sight. I said, "Honey," and Liz looked into the sky, sucked in her breath, squealed and leaned into me. "I've dreamt of this moment," she whispered. "I've fucking dreamt of it." The driver pulled up to the curb and I paid him. He pointed toward our hotel, which was just a few hundred yards away, and I nodded to tell him OK. Then I joined Liz, who was staring up at the faces. "There they are," I said, which was dumb.

The faces, I should note, looked really angry. I don't think they were frowning at *us*, per se, but you couldn't tell for sure.

Then a woman with a dog walked by, pointed at the faces, and pointed at us. I nodded and gave her a thumbs up. Meanwhile, Liz took out her phone. "So here we are in Chiba," she told it. "Right near what is called the Rinko Promenade. And look!" She held up her phone. "Who's that, Chris?"

I smiled into the camera.

"That's us!" said Liz. Take a look at that video now, though, and you can see how pissed off the faces look.

"What do you think, Chris?" Liz asked me.

I turned to the faces. "Hello us," I said.

And then all of a sudden I could hear a grinding in the sky. On the video, you can see me flinch and look up. "What's that sound?" I said.

"What sound?" said Liz.

Then I realized: it was the Liz-face. She was snarling. Then, just as Liz turned to look up at her, SkyLiz closed her eyes and head-butted SkyChris. "Oh!" shouted Liz, and she turned off her phone. What happened next was, the me-face shook off the hit and lunged at the Liz-face. "Oh buddy," I said.

But the Liz-face was ready for him. When he got close she opened her mouth, grabbed his nose in her teeth, and bit down. Blood fell from his face; some of it landed on Liz and me, some on a nearby tree.

"Shit!" I shouted.

The me-face recoiled and howled.

"Stop it!" shouted Liz at her face. "Why are you doing this?"

The Liz-face hissed and sped toward the me-face again. I heard the sound of a giant nose breaking, and I took Liz's hand and ran for cover. We didn't even grab our luggage. Liz sobbed all the way up to our room, where we opened the shade just in time to see Liz's face kill my face—she roared in victory as SkyChris collapsed on the treebelt.

On TV, meanwhile, faces were killing other faces by the thousands—these tiny floating wars were happening all over the world. We tried to get out of Chiba—to go home early—but all of the flights were grounded during the massacres. The fighting continued for the next nine days, most of which we spent in the hotel room either watching TV or fighting. When we finally got back home, Liz was morose for weeks. So was I. Sure, I drank more. I ate more too. Who didn't?

When the sky-violence finally stopped, the fifty or so faces that were left floated to far-off places, miles away from other faces that might attack them. So far as I know, they'll hiss and scowl if anyone approaches them. Now you rarely see a face anymore. Around here it happens once a year tops—seeing a face is like a holiday.

I don't mind admitting that I felt lonely when the faces left us; I think a lot of people did. I guess I thought for a while that they cared about us—that they were watching out for us. Even now, sometimes Liz and I will be working late in the afternoon and I'll look out over a rooftop and see what I think for a second is an eye in the sky. It never is, though: it's just a strange cloud, or the sun glinting off a building in a weird way, or a floater in my vision.

But then, right at that moment, there's that voice in my head—the one I've heard all my life, but only recently started listening to—reminding me that everything smiles. A tree; the breeze; the downspout of a gutter—the whole world is grinning at you. I don't even care if that's true—I'm going to believe it is anyway.

C.B.U.

I went to Christopher Boucher School because I wanted to be the best Christopher Boucher I could be. I'd been trying and failing at being Boucher for so long! My whole life, in fact. Right before she left Liz asked me: "Just who do you think you are?" And I really had no idea how to answer that question. I should have said something like "I'm Christopher Gerard Victor Boucher!", but instead I said something cruel and vulgar that I now regret.

For some reason, though, the option of going back to school didn't occur to me for the longest time. Sure, I would drive by these schools—Rev Morkan School, T'lur Academy, O'Malley Institutes—or I'd see their commercials on TV, but I never really gave them much thought. It wasn't until I found myself living in the tiny Bay State rooming house in Coolidge, Massachusetts, with no prospects and severe anxiety, that I realized I'd lost sight of myself — that something needed to change.

So I applied to CBU—and received a rejection two months later. "We are sorry to inform you," the email read, "that you have not been accepted to Christopher Boucher University for the fall 2017 semester. We appreciate your interest, though, and we wish you the best of luck in your future Boucher endeavors." I reapplied again the following year, and this time I was put on the wait list. And then someone must have dropped out or something, because a few weeks later I was accepted. How to pay for it, though? I'd been turned down for a scholarship, and didn't have a pot to piss in by that point.

But then, as luck would have it, my mother died, and even though she loathed me she left me a few bucks in her will. And since I knew she hated the idea of my enrolling at Boucher U.— "What can *they* teach you that I didn't?" she'd asked me once. "Um, how to be a good *person?*" I replied.—it seemed like fate that, ha ha, now she was paying for it. So I enrolled at CBU, ordered my textbooks, and rode the bus out to the campus—a five-building setup in East Coolidge, Massachusetts—for the first day of classes.

It took me a few minutes of wandering through the Sumner building before I found my classroom; when I finally did, I saw that it was already filled with Christopher Bouchers. I took an empty seat in the back and looked around. I knew one or two of these guys: Two rows up on the left was a Boucher I'd gone to high school with. Once, when I was thirteen, he beat the shit out of me for no reason at all. That was during my claymation phase, when I was spending all my free time in the public access television station. I was walking out of the studio one day and Boucher and four other guys were waiting for me. I could still remember his boot crashing down on my modeling clay. Now he'd gotten fat and gone bald; so had I. He turned and nodded to me, and I nodded back.

Then a man stepped into the room and strode to the front. Was *that* a Christopher Boucher? I wasn't sure at first—he was way more handsome than any Boucher I'd ever seen. Then— you'll never believe this—he addressed the class in *French*!

"*Bonjour,*" he said, in this silky baritone voice, "*et bienvenue à Christopher Boucher Université. Je m'appele Christopher Boucher, et je suis le professeur pour cette classe.*" Holy Jesus was I impressed.

Now, I am not normally a good student—or a good employee, *or* a good husband, or a good *anything* (unless eating chips is a thing, in which case I am very, very good)—but I studied hard at CBU. I read my textbook, *Christopher Boucher for Beginners*, all the way through twice. I learned everything about myself: my height (five nine); my weight (175); my various health problems (ulcerative colitis, obsessive compulsive disorder, allergies to tree fruits, pollen, and dust mites). I studied every chart and graph—the illustration of my receding hairline; a timeline of my failures—as closely as I could. And for the first time in my life, I really started to *get it*—to understand my faults and flaws. My selfishness. My narcissism. To overcome these problems, I worked with an entire team of Christopher Bouchers, some of whom were very tough on me. When I first met with my personal trainer, Coach B, I arrived at the track for our training session and he shook his head disgustedly and said, "Boy, are *you* out of shape!"

"Well," I said. "I'm forty-three. My metabolism—"

"Metabolism schmetabolism," he said.

"My face *is* a little fuller than it used to be," I admitted, "but if I untuck my shirt—"

He clapped his hands. "Less talking more moving, tubby. Let's start with a quick six."

"Six what?" I said.

He crossed his arms.

"*Miles?*" I said.

"Keep stalling and I'll make it seven."

I ran two miles, after which I stopped and collapsed on the grass. I seriously thought I was dying—everything was blue. Coach B leaned over me. "What the fuck is this?" he shouted.

"I'm—seeing blue," I gasped.

"I don't give a shit *what* color you're seeing," he said. "Get your ass up!"

I shook my head. "I can't," I said.

"*Can't* is not a word I know. Does it mean, I want to run eight miles instead of six?"

Weeping, I stumbled to my feet.

I also met with a psychiatrist—a Dr. Christopher Boucher—who tried to help me with OCD, anxiety, and my poor self-image. During our second meeting, I mentioned my writing and Dr. B leaned forward in his office chair. "I'm glad you brought that up," he said. "I've been meaning to ask you about it."

"Ask me about what?"

The doctor pulled out copies of my novels and put them on the table.

"Oh Jesus," I said.

The doctor pointed at the books. "Are all these stories true?"

"Of course they are," I said.

"Even the one about you killing a man?"

"I didn't kill him," I said. "He fell. It was an accident."

Dr. B. picked up *How to Keep Your Volkswagen Alive*. "And this person _____, the set designer. Is he an alter ego?"

I shook my head. "We used to work together is all."

Then the doctor picked up *Big Giant Floating Head*. "I found this one particularly sad," he said.

"Good," I said. "It's supposed to be sad."

The doctor's eyes narrowed. "You don't seem to like talking about your work," he said.

I shrugged.

"Let me just ask you one more question, then." Dr. B. opened the book and flipped to a page that he'd marked with a sticky note. "Is this an accurate portrayal of your mother?"

I nodded. "She hated me, too," I said.

"How could your own *mother* hate you?"

I held out my hands. "Isn't that obvious?"

Two weeks later, Dr. B took me and some other Bouchers out to the dumpster behind the office. "Now," he said to us all. "I want each one of you to lick this dumpster."

"What?" said one Christopher Boucher.

"No fucking way," said another Boucher, who I think was from Brattleboro.

"Oh no oh no oh no," said a third Boucher.

But Dr. B was firm; he stood next to each one of us and repeated the challenge. The first Boucher started crying and ran inside, but the second one actually leaned forward and touched his tongue to the rusty green metal. "Yack," he said, and spat.

By the time Dr. B got to me I was visibly shaking. "Chris?" he said. Then he pointed to the side of the dumpster, which was about a foot from my face. "Go ahead."

I just stood there shivering.

"What are you afraid of?" said Dr. B.

"Getting sick," I blurted.

"Right," he said. "That's a core issue for you. Can you put words to it?"

"I imagine dying," I blurted. "With no one around me—dying alone."

"But it's a distorted fear," he said. "And we're going to conquer it, right here and now."

"I can't," I told the doctor.

"Chris, you know very well that the odds of getting sick from this exercise are minimal. And that there's *always* a chance of getting sick. Right?"

I nodded.

He took another step closer to me. "Do you want to be a good Christopher Boucher, or the *best* Christopher Boucher?"

"The best Christopher Boucher," I said.

"Then lick this dumpster," he said.

I leaned forward and licked the dumpster.

On Tuesdays and Thursdays I met with a relationship specialist, a suave ponytailed Boucher who counseled me on being a better romantic partner. During the first session, he thumbed through my chart and said, "So you're married."

"No," I said.

"It says here you are," said Boucher.

"We're getting a divorce," I stated flatly.

Boucher's face darkened. "I'm very sorry to hear that, Chris." He made a note on his tablet. "Well, let's do a hypothetical then. Say you meet someone—someone new—and you want to get to know her better, to ask her out for coffee. What would you say?"

"I would say what I always say. 'I love you. I love you I love you.'"

"I mean when you've just met her," he said.

"Me too," I said. "I'd say 'I love you like a suitcase.'"

"Try something more subtle," he said.

"'I love you like a backpack.'"

The therapist stared at me.

I had a ways to go, but I made good progress that first semester. I learned to be kinder, more considerate, and less selfish. Plus I started eating better, dropped seven pounds, and developed some helpful techniques to boost my self-confidence and curb my anxiety.

One day in November, though, I was sitting in Get Taller! class when I noticed several empty seats in the front. Where was Boucher from Greenwich, and St. Louis Boucher? I asked the guy next to me what was going on; another Boucher had dropped out, he said. "*Another* Boucher?" I whispered.

"That's three in one month," he said.

A week or so later, we were informed by email that the professor who taught my Do Your Part! class would not be returning. The rumor around campus was that he took another job. "Another job?" I asked Ontario Boucher when he told me. "Where?"

"As a newspaper reporter, I heard," Ontario Boucher said. Sure enough, I opened *The Daily Wheel* the next day and saw my old professor's byline:

WORST LANGUAGE FLU IN YEARS, MAYOR SAYS
by CHRISTOPHER BOUCHER

Just two days after that, I rushed into Advanced Shutting Up and found Dean Boucher and Provost Boucher huddled at the front of the classroom. As soon as I sat down they turned to face the students. "Good morning everyone," said Dean Boucher.

"Good morning," the Christopher Bouchers replied.

"I've got some challenging news, which I know you might

find disappointing. Even so," said the Dean, holding out a fist, "I know you'll be Christopher Bouchers about it—that you'll keep your chins up and shoulder this like men."

"Shoulder *what?*" said Holyoke Boucher.

"Team," said Provost Boucher, stepping forward, "we're here to tell you that this school has been sold to Edgar O'Malley Institutes."

"What?" said a Boucher from the back of the room.

"No you did *not,*" said Christopher Boucher.

I looked over at the other Coolidge Boucher—we'd become friends by now—and he shook his head grimly.

"In this challenging financial time," said Dean Boucher, "we just can't afford to be second-tier. You've no doubt noticed that we lost several students this semester, and that Professor Boucher left us midway through the term."

"Believe me, Team," said the Provost, "when I say that we've done everything possible to remain viable. But there is just not enough interest in Christopher Boucher out there. His story's just not that compelling."

"But we can change that, can't we?" said Flagstaff Boucher. "Isn't that what you're *teaching* us?"

"Yes, of course," the Provost said. "Ultimately, though, we want what's best for you—"

"And for the school as well," said Dean Boucher.

"—and we think it's better for you long term if you are *not* Christopher Boucher," said the Provost.

The Bouchers began buzzing—muttering to each other and twisting in their seats. Then Tacoma Boucher raised his hand and said, "So, what—we're all *O'Malleys* now?"

"Hey personally, I'd *love* to be an O'Malley," said another Boucher.

"Who *is* O'Malley, anyway?" said the Boucher behind me.

I scoffed at the question. Edgar O'Malley was only Coolidge's most well-known restaurateur, the owner of seven gourmet organic restaurants. I'd once read an article on him in *The Wheel*: O'Malley was a "humanist," whatever that is, and an alternate on the 1994 Olympic Luge Team. He'd also written a collection of creative nonfiction.

"In answer to your question, Christopher," said the Dean, "we'll begin implementing the O'Malley Curriculum immediately."

"I know this is a bump in the road, folks," said the Provost. "But it's for the best. You're going to be much happier as Edgar O'Malleys."

That very afternoon we were given new student IDs, plus a new textbook, *Being Your Best Edgar*, by Edgar O'Malley, and a new course roster. And it soon became clear why O'Malley's schools were so popular: the curriculum was thorough, rigorous, and nearly foolproof. For us, it revealed the subtle but insistent flaws we'd fostered as Christopher Bouchers: the hidden sorrows at their core, the persisting anxieties that remained for even the best and brightest of them. O'Malley's courses—"Life Is a Kitchen"; "Every Moment Is a Performance"; "Be a Fucking MAN Already"—left no room for such faults. To assure lifelong self-confidence, for example, we began each morning with Mirror Drills, during which we'd stand tall in the Confidence Studio and face our reflections. Then we'd say, "I'm Edgar O'Malley—it's so nice to meet you," and extend our hand for a handshake.

"Louder!" boomed Provost O'Malley.

"I'M EDGAR O'MALLEY—IT'S SO NICE TO MEET YOU!" we shouted.

We did two hundred of these each day, and soon we *were* Edgar O'Malleys and it *was* so nice to meet you. After three more years of this, I'm sure we would have emerged not as less-anxious, slightly-taller Bouchers, but as handsome chef-author-athletes. And just two months into that spring semester, the school was thriving again—registration was up, and two new O'Malleys were hired: Edgar O'Malley, Esquire, who taught our Sue or Be Sued course, and Edgar O'Malley, M.D., to teach Sickness Is a Myth.

But I didn't care if the O'Malley Method *was* perfect—I missed being Christopher Boucher. And sometime that spring, a few of us—myself and two other O'Malleys—started meeting outside the new state-of-the-art luge track to smoke ciga-rettes and eat chips. And it turned out that they hated the new program as much as I did. "That fuckin' *O'Malley*, man?" said Pensacola O'Malley. "The way he talks to me?"

"Which one?" said Utica O'Malley.

"Gym O'Malley," said Pensacola. "He acts like he *invented* sit-ups. It's like, I work out *too*, OK? I was working out as *Boucher*."

"Fucking jerks," Utica O'Malley said.

A few weeks before the end of the semester, the three of us dropped out. Our hearts just weren't in it. For better or worse, we went back to being Christopher Bouchers. From then on the drop-out O'Malleys met once every few weeks in a bar or at one of our houses, where we really Bouchered it up: we'd drink a bunch of beers, eat a few bags of chips while watching a bad movie, fall asleep on the couch. We weren't impressive and no one loved us. We were fat, anxious, divorced. We weren't even nice to *each other*; once, we locked Christopher Boucher out of Christopher Boucher's apartment for no good reason. "Guys?" he said, knocking at the door. "It's Chris. Christopher Boucher." But we just ignored him until he went away. Sure, we talked about changing—going back to school, enrolling to be someone else—but I doubt any of us thought that was really going to happen. Deep in his heart, I think every Christopher Boucher out there knew it was all downhill from here.

SLIPPERY

Once everything became slippery. Suddenly I couldn't hold my wife's hand, couldn't grasp the chess pieces when we played. I couldn't tie my shoes, couldn't grip the handle of my office door at work. The entire world turned wet and slick. At first it was a physical slipping, then a mental one as well. I forgot my wife's birthday. I was suspended from work at the Department of Fiction for two weeks and I had no idea why. I came home from the supermarket and my wife had a duffel bag packed. "Fuck *you*," she said, and she brushed past me, closed herself into her Honda and pulled out of the driveway. I ran after her. "Liz, what? Liz? Liz!"

I went to the doctor and he took the top of my head off and looked around. "Hm," he said. "Hm what?" I said. His pliers felt cold inside my mind. "Well," he said, "I can adjust the wire that controls your relationship to the external—" "OK," I said. "There's a but," he said. "OK," I said. "The but is," he said, "your mind may overcompensate." "Meaning what," I said. "Meaning," he said, "that you might have the opposite problem." I tried to deduce what he was saying without actually saying it. "That things won't be slippery enough?" I said. "Exactly," he said. "That things will stick."

Which is exactly what happened. I experienced one very good day, the best day of my life, maybe, during which I could hold the things I wanted to and let go of them when I was ready to. When I woke up the next morning, though, the bed sheets stuck to me. I didn't think too much of it, but then I tried to eat a piece of toast and it stuck to my chin. An old girlfriend called me and said she was coming over, and by two p.m. we were married. She clung to me as we walked toward the subway so we could catch a plane and begin our honeymoon. As we were crossing the street, though, a car screamed toward us. Its brakes squealed but it slammed right into my rib. It was a Honda—Liz's Honda. The car stuck to me. Inside it, Liz screamed, "Honey! Let go of that woman!"

I called the doctor and told him I needed to see him immediately. I arrived at his office with a piece of toast stuck to my face, my arm around my new wife, my old wife's Honda attached to my abdomen. It was a struggle to fit into the examination room!

The doctor came in with his chart. He wrote down the make and model of the car. Then he interviewed Liz and took my new wife's name. "Hm," he said. "Hm what?" I said. "Hm as in, I think your brain is overcompensating. My diagnosis is, things are now *sticking* to you." "I agree with your diagnosis," I told him. "So what now?" "Well," he said, "you may have to choose." I asked him, "Why can't you just scale it back a smidge?" "That's what I tried to do last time," he said. "I can adjust it again, but I think you may have to choose which you'd prefer. Do you want your life to be too sticky or too slippery?"

I didn't really even have to think about it. "Slippery," I said.

"Honey, no!" both wives said in unison. "Honeys, it has to be this way," I told them. "I'd rather be nothing in this world than go through it attaching myself to everything." I turned back to the doctor. "Do it," I said. "Change me back."

The doctor opened my head and made the adjustment. It only took five minutes. As soon as he'd finished, the car dislodged itself from me and the new wife divorced me. Liz gave me the finger, pulled a U-turn, and sped the Honda out of the doctor's office.

The piece of toast fell off my face and onto the floor of the office. I tried to pick it up, but I could not—it was too slippery. The doctor took pity on me, picked up the toast and held it for me. I was so hungry—I felt like I hadn't eaten in months.

"Go ahead," he said. "Eat."

He held the toast to my lips. I took a bite from it.

"Thank you," I said. "Hey," he said. "That's what I'm here for."

LADY WITH INVISIBLE DOG

I met the Lady with the Invisible Dog about a year after my uncle's death, at the same exact time that I was rustle-tussling with a man called "the Narrator." This was back in 1999, years before I met Liz. I'd taken the money that my uncle had left me and opened up a bookstore, and this Narrator—a blond-haired, moustache-and-muscle fellow from Blix—started harassing me and making all of these threats. At first I didn't take them seriously, but then my co-worker Boris Sarah clarified for me exactly how troublesome this Narrator character might become for us. I asked Boris Sarah what to do.

"Make friends with him!" Boris Sarah replied. "Tell him you see his point! Apologize for your rude behavior!"

"Apologize!" I said. "Formally?"

"I don't think you appreciate the severity of this situation," Boris Sarah said.

So the next day I walked across the street to the Coolidge Department of Apologies (CDA) to fill out the form. I'd filed apologies before (lots of them, in fact), so I knew how to do it. I walked up to the second floor of City Hall, found the table of blank forms located outside the CDA office, and filled out the form that said "Submission for Formal Apology." In the space where it asked what I was apologizing for, I wrote down exactly what the Narrator had told me, in the same exact words he'd spat at me during our tiff in my store a few days earlier: From a certain perspective, my business could be seen as disrespectful to his enterprise—as a threat to his livelihood, even. I wrote that maybe we could sit down over a beer and talk about our differences, maybe even find a way to work together.

I completed the form and brought it up to the window, but the lady behind the glass—a woman in her twenties, with short, straight blond hair, a red-and-white-checkered shirt, smooth sunrise skin, and a face like a television tuned to just the right channel—said, "Oh, I'm sorry."

"I'm sorry?" I said.

"This isn't the wrong form," she said.

"*Isn't* the wrong form?" I said.

"I mean, it *is* the wrong form," she said, smiling. "Is the wrong form." That's how she spoke, like a crumbly sidewalk.

"I'm sorry," I said, "I must have grabbed the wrong one—"

"Actually, we don't accept printed forms anymore."

"So how do I apologize?"

"The new form is online," she said.

"Online?" I asked.

"Yeah. On the web."

"I'm sorry? What web?"

She squinted (so she could see my face better, I assumed). "The internet," she said.

"What's—the—"

"You just go to the CDA home page and the form's available as a PDF file."

I shook my head—I had no idea what she was talking about.

"You just print it out," she said.

I was still confused, and so I did that thing that I sometimes do—that I'd been doing a lot since my uncle's death, actually—which is, I just left; I just turned around in the middle of her sentence and walked back through the hallway, down the stairs and out into the cold, cold, cold, cold, cold.

· ✦ ·

I went back to the store, which was called Tomorrow Books. That's what we sold—books you'd never seen before. Some of them were made of paper, and resembled traditional books, but most were completely new—they were made of wood, or wire, or cloud, or light, or suggestions. We even sold books made of missing, like this one. Some of the books told stories and some didn't—sometimes the book *was* the story. At that point, though, we were hardly selling any books—maybe two or three on a good week. During our first few months in business almost all of our funding came from the money my uncle Sun—the only person in the world who'd ever cared about me—left me when he died.

Sunny had known that he was dying—he was getting lighter and lighter—so during his last weeks he made sure to put all his affairs in order. He put my inheritance in a bank account, and in that same bank he left some valuables in a safe-deposit box along with a note that said, *Winner* (that's what he called me): *This is a lot of money. Don't waste it on something stupid. I mean it. Love, Sunny.*

It wasn't long after that—after his death—that I tried writing my first story. The story was dead and deformed, but I told myself I'd continue writing. I promised myself I'd find a way to capture all that missing—an unloveable father, a mother who never loved *me*, an uncle who I would have given anything to see again—and put it on the page.

Anyhoo, it was me and Boris Sarah at the store, and between the two of us we made most of the books that we sold (save for an occasional tomorrowish book written by one of our favorites—Reichle, Toom, etc.).

When I got back to the store, Boris Sarah was building a steel book. I walked in and asked, "Have you ever heard of something called the internet?"

"The who?" said Boris Sarah.

·✦·

But who did I see later that afternoon? While working in the store?

The Lady from the CDA! She was walking by the store and she saw me working—I was building a book made from bread. The Lady knocked on the window and waved, and a minute or so later she came inside, where she waved at me again. She was all bundled up in a red coat and a red hat.

I pushed my bookmaking goggles up onto my forehead. "Hey," I said. I held out my arms. "Welcome to Tomorrow Books!"

"You work here?"

"This is my store," I said. "Me and Boris Sarah back there."

Boris Sarah waved, and the Lady from the CDA waved back.

"I'm sorry about before," she said. "With the form."

"Not your fault," I said.

"But I can show it to you, how to fill it out, if you want."

"Oh—yeah," I said. "Great. Right now?"

She nodded.

I told Boris Sarah that I was going out again, and I stood up from my worktable.

"I'm Molly, by the way," said the Lady from the CDA.

"Christopher," I told her.

She nodded and smiled. "Cool," she said. Then she turned and walked outside, and I followed.

And that's when I noticed the leash.

She'd tied the leash up to a parking meter, but there was nothing at the end of it. It was just an empty leash!

Molly untied the leash and we started walking. The leash floated out in front of her, zipping to the left and to the right. I heard the tiny clanging of a bell. I didn't know what to make of what I was seeing, but I didn't want to be rude so I didn't say anything.

Molly walked me down to a storefront that read "JavaNet Café."

"Oh yeah," I said, "I've heard about this place. They have magazines, right?"

She asked, "Have you ever been inside?"

"I haven't," I said. She tied the empty leash to a bike rack and led me through the heavy glass doors of the café.

The inside of the JavaNet had hardwood floors and brick walls and counters made of copper. Molly led me past a rack of magazines on the left and a coffee bar on the right. Toward the back of the café, a grouping of tables held big monitors and keyboards. "These are computers," she said.

"Sure," I said, "I know what a computer is."

"But not the internet?"

"I remember you mentioning that," I said. "I don't know what that is."

She sat down at the chair and typed some information on the keyboard. Within a minute or two, the printer in the corner of the café hummed to life and gave birth to a single sheet of paper. The Lady grabbed the newborn paper and placed it in my arms. "Here you go," she said.

"Jesus," I said. "Christ. It's like a home printing press!"

"Are you really not familiar with this stuff?"

I shook my head. I might have known about it at some point, but if so that information had disappeared on me. This was happening to me more and more these days: My memories burrowed and hid in my mind; basic information was somehow blocked from me; my thoughts wandered far away where I couldn't reach them. "I don't know about any of this stuff," I said.

"Because people sometimes kid me, and I don't know that they're doing it."

"I'm really not kidding you," I said.

Then there was a moment of silence, during which I studied Molly's face while she studied mine. Her eyes, I discovered, were tunnels, and those tunnels led to other eyes further back in her skull—which, I could tell, was where the thinking happened.

"I really appreciate your help," I said. "How can I thank you?"

"No problem," Molly said.

"The least I could do is write a story about you."

"A story?" she asked.

"A *tomorrow* story," I said.

• ✦ •

This is that story.

Or at least, one revision of it. When I write the final version, I'm going to begin it like this:

Her name was Molly, and she worked at the CDA.

Isn't that a good first line?

• ✦ •

I thanked Molly and told her that I'd fill out the form and bring it by the next day. And I did—the next morning I walked into the CDA office and Molly was sitting behind the glass. Her hair was like a crisscross quilt of corn.

"Hey—good morning," she said.

"I came by with the form," I said, and handed it over the counter.

She read it over. "Wow," she said. "You threatened to close down this guy's business?"

"Not exactly," I said. "It's a long story."

"Does he own a bookstore?"

"No," I said, "but he's in the story business."

Molly stared at me. Then she said, "I'm just about to go on break and take Bon Jovi for a walk. Do you want to come?"

I didn't completely follow what she was saying—who was Bon Jovi?—but I said, "Sure."

She slid the glass window closed, and a minute later stepped

— 47 —

out of the office and into the hallway. She was holding the same empty leash. This time, though, she let the leash go, and I saw it move, on its own, toward me. Then I felt something warm against my leg. Molly said, "Have I introduced you two?"

· ✦ ·

And it was then that I realized that her dog was invisible. She never said as much, but I deduced it. I bent down to pet the dog, and I said, "Nice to meet you—"

"Bon Jovi," she said.

"Nice to meet you, Bon Jovi."

· ✦ ·

And everything started making sense in my mind.

We walked over to Coolidge College, past the library and toward the greenhouse and the man-made pond. Molly didn't say much at first, but then she said, "So you write the books at Tomorrow Books?"

"I build them—some of them."

"How do you know how to do that?"

"My father was in stories," I said. "The rest of it I taught myself."

We walked down the hill to Outlaw Pond, and Bon Jovi ran to the edge of the water where he peed and pooped. Which looked very strange, by the way—the pee and poop seemed to appear out of nowhere.

Molly must have seen me staring at her dog because she said, "What."

"What?" I said. "Nothing."

"Your face is sort of hard for me to see," she said. "I can't tell what that look means."

"Was Bon Jovi always invisible?" I asked.

Molly shook her head. "He was opaque as a puppy, and became translucent at about ten months."

I nodded. Then I said, "Don't some people say invisibility's contagious?"

"That's total bullcrap," Molly said. "Scientists in Europe have proved that it's genetic."

"I've heard that theory, too," I said.

"Why—does it worry you?"

I said no, but the truth was that it did and it didn't. Part of me was nervous about it (especially when I remembered that invisible dogs were illegal in some states—though not in Massachusetts, obviously). Another part of me was okay with it, though, because I already felt invisible sometimes. I'd felt that way since I was a child. Sometimes it seemed like people had trouble seeing me, reading my face. When I'd heard the theory about the invisibility gene, I wondered if maybe I carried it. It wouldn't surprise me; I sort of remembered something that my mom told me about an invisible great aunt.

And something sort of like invisibility had ruined a previous relationship. My girlfriend and I'd only been dating a month when she started complaining that I was talking too quietly. I'd say something to her and she'd say, "What?" I'd say it again. "What?" she'd say.

It was like my *voice* became invisible. And as far as I knew, those kinds of distortions sometimes preceded translucency.

After two more months of that, my girlfriend came over

to my apartment one night and broke up with me. I objected weakly but she couldn't hear me. She said she was sorry and gave me a hug, and then I did that thing that I do—I left. I walked out of our apartment with no keys, no money, and no change of clothes.

· ✦ ·

And that was the last relationship I'd had. So it was nice to walk around the campus with Molly and her invisible dog. I didn't mind that we didn't say much to each other—the fact that she could hear me was a birthday in itself.

As we walked back toward downtown, I asked Molly about her job and she said that she'd been working for the CDA for about two years. She said that she liked working for the city, but that she hoped to eventually work in federal apologies. "That's where the real money is," she said.

"It seems like a good field," I said. "More and more people are apologizing these days."

"That's why I got into it," she said. "We had ten percent more apologies at the CDA last year than we did the year before."

"Wow," I said.

When we reached the store, I bent down to say goodbye to Bon Jovi, and his invisible tongue licked my hand. Then I stood up and Molly's face changed channels to a bright smile. "Tomorrow?"

"Sure," I said.

· ✦ ·

The next morning, about twenty minutes before we opened, the Narrator opened up the locked front door of our store and stood in the center of the carpet. "Morning, ladies and gents," he said.

I stood up from my workbench, and so did Boris Sarah. "We're closed," said Boris Sarah.

"Not to me, you're not," said the Narrator.

The Narrator had first appeared in my store a few months earlier, during our grand opening—he spent hours browsing through the shelves, and then he approached my worktable and asked to speak to a manager. "We're both managers," Boris Sarah told him.

The Narrator introduced himself—he handed me a business card that said "The Narrator" along with a phone number and a mailing address. The Narrator told us that he lived in Blix, and that he'd narrated more than a hundred books. "I've been looking around your store," he said, "and frankly I'm a little concerned." I asked him why and he said, "None of these books have narration." He pulled a book off the shelf and flipped through the pages. "I mean, where are the words?"

"That one doesn't have words," said Boris Sarah.

"What does it do, then?"

"It just hums."

"The book—hums?"

"Sure," Boris Sarah said.

"Where's the story?"

"There is no story," I said.

Then another customer came in with a return, and the Narrator waited for a few minutes and then left in a huff. He returned again the following day and confronted me with the same complaints—that my books needed narrators. "Listen," he said, "we have a real problem here, you and I. Western Mass. is not a big place—there's only so much business for booksellers like us."

"This really isn't a good time for me to talk," I said, sitting down at my typewriter. "I'm right in the middle of a project."

"What I'm saying is, the more people buy your books, the less people buy mine. You can understand my concern, right?"

I should have said yes, that I understood. I should have said that there was room enough for both of our books on the shelves. But I didn't—I was trying to work, and frustrated that I couldn't, so I said, "Every business that I know of faces competition. Now are you going to buy something or aren't you?"

The Narrator crossed his arms. "Excuse me?"

"You heard me," I said.

"Am I going to buy something?" The Narrator looked shocked. Then he smiled tentatively and said, "What I want to know is, how are you going to write books without a typewriter?"

"What are you talking about?" said Boris Sarah. "Christopher has a typewriter—he's typing on it right now!"

"You sure that's your typewriter?" the Narrator said to me. "Because it looks an awful lot like mine."

I looked up at him. "My uncle gave me this typewriter," I said.

"But now I think you're giving it to me."

"What?" I said.

The Narrator closed his eyes. In a voice that sounded like caramel he said, "The next day, the Narrator visited Tomorrow Books to talk some sense into Christopher and Boris Sarah. But they wouldn't listen."

"What are you doing?" said Boris Sarah.

But I understood what he was doing: he was narrating.

The Narrator, his eyes still closed, said, "But then Christopher did something strange: he unplugged his typewriter and gave it to the Narrator."

As if under a spell, my body began to move. Without wanting to, I unplugged my electric typewriter and handed it over to the Narrator.

The Narrator opened his eyes and feigned surprise. "Wow—thanks very much," he said.

As soon as I put the typewriter in his hands I reached to grab it back, but the Narrator pulled it away. I began to realize who this guy was, what I'd done. "Listen," I said. "I didn't mean to be rude. It's just that we're a new business, and—"

"You know what?" said the Narrator. "You just pissed off the wrong Narrator." Then he closed his eyes and said, "The door of Tomorrow Books swung open and the Narrator stormed out."

The door of the store swung open and the Narrator walked out, carrying my uncle's typewriter in his arms.

· ✦ ·

Now the Narrator stood in my store, grinning at me. "I just *love* my new typewriter," he said. "But you know what I was thinking? It occurred to me this morning that maybe I need a nice worktable to go with it."

"Listen," I said, holding out my hands, "I think we just got off on the wrong foot."

"Bet your ass we did," said the Narrator. "You wanted competition? You got it."

"Wait a second," I said. "Did you get my apology?"

"What apology?" he said.

"I filed an apology."

"Formally?"

"Yeah," I said.

"You paid the fee?"

I nodded.

I could tell he was surprised. "You lying to me?" he said incredulously.

"Of course not," I said.

"I haven't received it," said the Narrator.

"It must be on its way then," I said.

"I'll check for it when I get home," said the Narrator. "And you'd better hope it's there—"

"It should have gotten to you yesterday," I said.

"—because I wouldn't want to have to come back here and tear your store apart," the Narrator said.

"I just have to think that there's a way to sort this out," I said.

Molly and I walked Bon Jovi every day at lunch and sometimes after work. We walked all around Coolidge: up to Magazine Street near Joe's; over to Inquiry Ave; around the corner to Masonic and the Masonic Café; up Route 9 to Demand and Crescent; across the street to Poutine Park; down to Molly's apartment on Conz Street; down Joy Blvd to the Memory of

Bread bakery; past _____'s house and onto Hawley; over to my apartment on South; once, on a weekend, all the way to the Statue of Coolidge.

· ✦ ·

And over time, Bon Jovi and I became friends.

After a few weeks of walks, Molly even started leaving Bon Jovi at the store with me. I guess he'd caused some trouble at the CDA when he started barking at co-workers and apologizers, and since we still weren't getting many customers at Tomorrow Books, I told Molly I could keep an eye on her dog.

Bon Jovi seemed to really like hanging out at the store—he used to sit on the floor near the word-forge, where it was warm. And sometimes I'd be binding, and I'd hear the bell on Bon Jovi's collar ring, and then I'd feel him nuzzle at my feet. I'd look down and see the leg of my pants imprinted where Bon Jovi was lying against my shin.

· ✦ ·

One day, maybe a month after I met Molly, she and I took Bon Jovi for a walk down by the airport and past the Fields of No. We took Bon Jovi off his leash and he ran into the woods. He liked to sneak up on squirrels, and you've never seen a squirrel run so fast as one being chased by an invisible dog. Molly and I walked down Last River Road until we came upon the memory of a house. We looked out past the house and toward the water behind it.

Molly said, "I love the fact of the river."

"The fact of the river?" I said.

"That it's right here, I mean."

"Yeah," I said. The air was delightfully cold. "Maybe we should buy this house, fix it up."

Molly looked at me with her blue eyes cloudy and her cloudy face. "With what money?"

"I have some money," I said.

"Who'd live here?" she said. "You or me?"

"We could both live here," I said.

Bon Jovi barked in the distance.

Molly leaned in. "It's just the memory of a house," she said. "Not a real house."

"It could be real, though."

She took my hand, smiled, and shook her head. "We couldn't live here," she said.

"Why not?"

Suddenly I was very nervous. When I looked into Molly's eyes—far back into them, into her eyes behind her eyes—I could tell that she wanted me to kiss her. But I was frozen; I couldn't move. This was maybe the only moment in my life when I wished for the Narrator—I wished he could have been there to close his eyes and say, "And then Molly and Christopher kissed."

Finally Molly said, "I've been looking for someone to like, or to love."

"You have?"

"Maybe that could be you."

A thought in my mind tripped and fell. "People get tired of me," I said.

"I won't," said Molly.

We stared at each other for a moment. Then Molly said, "Wouldn't this be a good time in the story for a kiss to happen?"

"I don't know," I said.

Molly leaned in and kissed me. I still try to remember it—how cold and soft her lips were. It wasn't a French-style kiss, either—it was a good old Coolidge-style kiss: short but nice.

· ✦ ·

But the very next day, something terrible happened while Boris Sarah and I were trying to move a very large book into the store. The book was called a Superbook, and it was nine feet wide and fifteen feet high, with pages made of Luaun. The damn book got stuck in the doorway while we were trying to move it in—it got lodged there and we couldn't budge it. Obviously very pissed, Boris Sarah swore and paced up and down the store. "What a waste of time this is," said Boris Sarah. "And do you really think we're ever going to sell this thing?"

"Are you kidding me?" I said. "These Superbooks are the next big thing! And we'll be the first store in Coolidge to carry them."

Finally we were able to get the book through the door, and we leaned it against a shelf of false calendars. Since Boris Sarah still seemed ticked off, I decided to take Bon Jovi for a walk. "Bon Jovi!" I called. I didn't hear his bell, so I called him again. When I still couldn't hear him I said, "Where's Bon Jovi?"

"Who?" said Boris Sarah.

"Molly's dog," I said.

"He's not here?" Boris Sarah looked around and then pointed to the back door. "Christopher," Boris Sarah said. "Could he have snuck out while we were moving in the Superbook?"

I called the dog's name again, and then I walked out into the alley. "Bon Jovi!" I shouted.

No Bon Jovi.

I called Molly at work, and she came right over—five minutes later she was standing in the bookstore, her eyes turnstiles. "Where did you last see him?" she asked.

"Right here," I said. "He was at my worktable."

"We propped open the door when we moved in that Superbook," said Boris Sarah.

"The book got stuck in the door, actually," I said.

"The what?" said Molly.

"The Superbook," said Boris Sarah, pointing to the giant book.

Molly turned to me and said, "You didn't put him on his leash?"

I didn't say anything.

"Christopher?"

"No, I didn't," I said.

Molly and I walked all over Coolidge—we searched Poutine Park, the Coolidge College campus, everywhere. We walked as far as the Fields of No, then turned back in the hopes that maybe Bon Jovi had returned to the store. Molly wouldn't speak to me—she just marched along in silence. "The fact that he's invisible makes this really difficult," I said, trying to ease the tension.

Molly glared at me. "That dog is a really good friend of mine," she said.

By the time we got back to Tomorrow Books we'd been walking for hours—it was almost six p.m., and completely dark. Molly's face was wet with tears when we pushed open the door of the bookstore.

And guess who was standing there. "Oh, great," I said.

"You fucking liar," said the Narrator.

· ✦ ·

"What will you take from me this time?" I asked.

"You're a liar—you never filed any apology," the Narrator said.

"I told you, I submitted it to the CDA," I said.

"Bullshit," he said.

"I swear to God I did," I said.

The Narrator's eyes narrowed. Then he closed his eyes and began to narrate. "Then, suddenly, for no apparent reason," the Narrator said, "Christopher punched himself in his own face."

My hand closed into a fist and I punched myself in my own face.

"Oh!" I said. "Ah!" My mind growled and my nose bled.

"How *dare* you lie to me," said the Narrator.

"I swear I did—I got the form online," I said.

"On-what?" said the Narrator.

"Online," I said. "Through the computer."

"What?"

I looked to Molly for help. Her face was cold.

The Narrator closed his eyes again and said, "And then, as if punching himself in the face wasn't bad enough, Christopher reached into his mouth, took hold of his own tooth, and began to pull."

And I did.

"Ah!" I screamed. "Please!" I begged.

"And slowly," the Narrator said, "Christopher pulled the tooth out."

I tried like hell to unclench my hand, to stop my arm from pulling, but I had no control over my body.

After a minute or two of pulling, the tooth came out. I almost blacked out from the pain. I shrieked and howled and wept. "I *did* submit it," I said through a bloody mouth. "I promise. Ask her," I said, and I pointed to Molly.

The Narrator and Molly looked at each other.

"Molly, tell him!"

Molly was focused on me. "You know what, Christopher? You deserve this."

"We'll find him, Molly," I mumbled, spitting blood.

"Find who?" the Narrator said.

"Her dog," I said.

"You had a responsibility—you were supposed to watch him," Molly said to me.

The Narrator pointed at me. "*Christopher* lost your dog?"

Molly nodded, and began to cry.

"He *is* invisible," I mumbled.

The Narrator's eyes were bright. He studied Molly's splotchy face; then he said to her, "What's your dog look like?"

"He's invisible," Molly said.

"What's his name?"

"Bon Jovi," she said.

The Narrator closed his eyes and said, "And then, much to everyone's surprise, Bon Jovi walked right up to the front door of Tomorrow Books. Christopher and—I'm sorry, what's your name?"

"Molly," she said.

"—Christopher and Molly heard the sound of paws at the front door," said the Narrator.

And right then we heard the jingling of a bell outside, and a scratching at the door.

Molly and the Narrator took Bon Jovi and they left my store. And that was the second- or third-to-last time I ever saw Molly; she didn't return my calls, and after a while I stopped trying to get in touch with her. I noticed her walking the empty leash across the street once or twice, but I never went over to talk to her, and she never came back into the store.

The Narrator did continue to come by, though not to harass me. He totally changed his tune toward me after I introduced him to Molly. She ended up choosing *him* to love, and together they made a lot of money in e-sales; they sold my typewriter and a bunch of the Narrator's books on the internet. Now they have a house in Blix.

Meanwhile, my face became harder and harder to see. Finally I went to my doctor, Doctor Ice, and he gave me some medication that stopped the invisibility from translucentizing my entire body. But there was nothing he could do about my face. People seemed to look past me even more than before. It was like every new person I met was my mother.

And they looked past my store, too. We struggled to stay afloat. Some of our customers were fascinated by the Superbook, but when I told them how much it cost they always left the store immediately.

The last time the Narrator came by Tomorrow Books, I asked him if maybe he'd consider giving me narration lessons. He scoffed. "No," he said.

"Why not?" I said.

"You're no narrator," he said, smirking.

"But maybe I could be," I said. Then I told him how much money we were losing every week. He listened intently, and then he actually apologized to me. "Six months ago that would have been music to my ears," he said, "but now—"

He stopped speaking, and seemed to wander in his thoughts for a moment. Then he closed his eyes and said, "Christopher felt sad about losing Molly, and about his invisible face, and with his store struggling it looked like all hope was lost."

"You can say that again," I said.

The Narrator kept his eyes closed. "But even if the Narrator never said as much, he felt optimistic about Christopher's chances."

"You do?" I said.

"Somewhere out there, on one page or another, was happiness with Christopher's name on it. The question was, would Christopher find it?"

"Yes," I promised. "I will."

"That kind of quest takes work," the Narrator said. "*Years* of searching, sometimes."

"I'll scour this entire *book* if I have to," I promised. "I'll do whatever it takes."

THE LANGUAGE ZOO

We were all really excited about the Grand Reopening of the Language Zoo. The renovation had been long overdue. The old zoo? Nothing more than a few caged metaphors and some humdrum local sentences lack-a-dairying on rocks. The new zoo, meanwhile, rallied to be one of the best in America, featuring language not seen anywhere else. So when they announced that admission would be free for the Grand Reopening, we knew we had to go.

That morning we drove out on Route 65, turned into a newly paved parking lot, locked our cars, and paraded through the front gate and into the Table of Contents. Everything about the new facility was stunning: the new walking paths white and clean, the attendants dressed in matching white shirts, the language separated from readers by glass and housed on climate-controlled pages. To our right walking in, we could see inferences in the trees and questions jumping in and out of a small pond. Next to these were strange, slithering adjectives, followed by prepositions hanging high in their cages or burrowing low in hollowed-out logs.

But it was so hot out that day, and after just a few minutes some of us were sweating through our clothes. We were also thirsty, and a few of us had to go to the bathroom. So we made our way to the Welcome Center, which held a small movie theater—*The History of Language in America* was playing when we peeked in—and a gift shop. We couldn't help ourselves: we bought keychains with replica language and books about the lives of famous words. Then, while sipping our lemonade and watching some tiny words swim in freshwater tanks, we noticed the sign for the special exhibit on endangered language. "Let's go see that," we decided. So we sucked the last drops of lemonade from our cups and walked back out onto the hot page.

Soon we reached the exhibit tent and joined the big giant line at the entrance. Some of us were irked that we had to wait. "How long is this going to take?" demanded a few. "Is all this waiting really worth it?" asked others. When we finally reached the tent entrance, we saw a list of rules: no food, alcohol, or flash photography. "All Cell Phones Must Be Turned Off," said the sign. "They Frighten the Language!" Some of us turned off our phones, but others scoffed at the warning. "Who's going to know one way or the other?" we asked ourselves.

Then we stepped into the tent. To our left we saw displays of prehistoric language—the imprints of old, strange, dead words on the page—and then, past that, really big words, some of the biggest in all of America (or so said the sign), which we huddled around and oohed and aahed at. We moved past laid-back double entendres and newborn irony, and then we saw a huge collection of rare sincerity behind thick glass dividers about forty feet away. We pushed our way toward those phrases. I saw "I miss you" walk past the glass, "I already felt invisible" cross behind it, and "I am so sad and lonely" crouching in the corner.

Attendants weaved through us, trying to keep us back from the glass. But the phrases were too amazing—we had to capture and share them. So one of us snuck our phone out of our pocket and took a picture, and then another one of us saw that and did the same—only, we forgot to turn off the flash this time. We all saw the burst of light from the flash—so did an attendant. "No pictures!" she shrieked. But those of us in the front couldn't even hear her, and meanwhile, another one of us had taken out our phone and started filming a video. Seeing the camera, though, a giant "What will you take from me this time?" bristled and paced behind the glass. "All phones turned *off*!" shouted another attendant. Some of us started looking for the exit—it was tremendously hot in the tent, and there were too many of us in there. Then one of us began pushing, and another pushed back, and soon there were waves of shoving among the crowd. Behind the glass, meanwhile, the language grew anxious, defensive; then the word "soulmate" locked letters with "lonely," and "never" reared up and roared at "forever."

"Back up!" shouted an attendant. "Don't press against the glass!"

"Keep moving!" shouted another attendant.

But we couldn't move—there was nowhere for us to go. It became difficult for us to breathe. Then we heard a rumble and looked up just in time to see "I am so sad and lonely" lower its head and crash against the glass, creating a spiderweb pattern over that entire paragraph.

"Out!" shouted one of the attendants. "Everyone out of the tent!"

"I am so sad and lonely" hit the glass again, and this time the pane shattered. Everyone shoved and clawed and ran, but the wild sincerity was too fast and powerful; the language moved among us, through us, over us. Suddenly we loved each other and missed each other and held each other in our hearts. We believed in each other and we knew we were supposed to spend the rest of our lives with each other. And then we *were* so sad and lonely. Some of us were crushed in the stampede; others were gored; others cowered behind the glass or dove behind the dead or the giant words in the adjacent exhibit. Zoo attendants arrived with brackets and parentheses, but by then it was too late: the language was gone—out of the tent and thundering through the zoo. We didn't yet realize how much havoc it would cause—that it would run wild through the novel, scare off existing names and phrases—but we already missed those moments: the times when we were in love, when we gave our hearts to each other, when we promised each other the world. Those that could ran to the edge of the tent just in time to see all those truths—"I miss you," "I will always love you," "How do I live without love?" and so many others—leap over the back fence of the zoo, run out of the story and jump off the page, then onto the adjacent pages and forward into the future. We watched them disappear, our hearts bitter with regret.

How do I live without love?

I'm so sad and lonely

Thank you. Thank you so much for everything

You are the most beautiful person I've ever seen

BODYWALL

Christopher woke up that morning with a new pressure in his head—a tension of some sort between his eyebrows and behind his ears. He stood up woozily, stumbled to the bathroom, and looked in the mirror. When he leaned forward, he could see a rectangle shape pressing outward at the center of his forehead.

"What *is* that?" said a thought in the right side of his brain.

"It's a wall," said a thought in the left side.

"What?" said a right-side thought.

"Yeah, it's the edge of a wall."

"I can't hear you—I can't make out what you're saying," said the right-thought.

"Dumbthought says what," said the left-thought.

"What?" said the right-thought.

"Nice one," said another left-thought, and the two high-fived.

It seemed like everyone was talking about walls that year. They'd built one between Coolidge and East Coolidge, for example, and now another one was going up in Blix.

Christopher found his cell phone and called his ex-wife. "Hey," Liz said.

"Listen," Christopher said. "Something weird is happening to me."

"Uh-huh," she said.

"I've got this protrusion on my forehead."

"Like a zit?"

"No," he said.

"Like a cyst or something?"

"It's—blocky. Like a—" He struggled to say it—"a wall."

"Jesus, Chris," she said.

"Should I call the doctor?"

"You call the doctor more than anyone I know," Liz said. "Didn't you call him last Friday?"

"I was itchy," Christopher said. "I thought I had bedbugs."

"It's probably just anxiety, Chris," Liz said. "Wait a day and see if it goes away."

Christopher called in sick to work and went back to bed. As he slept, though, he dreamt two dreams simultaneously. One was about a cow sitting at a table at a restaurant. That was the whole dream: the cow opened up the menu and read through it thoughtfully.

The other dream was about Liz. She lived in West Geryk now, but in the dream she and Christopher were back in their old house in Coolidge and Christopher was telling Liz how much he missed her. "I miss the arguments, the dumb little meaningless moments. I even miss this broken-down house."

"But we're in the house right now," Liz said. Then she turned her head and said, "Hey—what's that?"

"What's *what*?" said dream-Christopher.

"That," she said. She pointed to their kitchen window. Instead of containing a view of their driveway, though, it showed a cow reading a menu.

"Oh, that's a different dream," said dream-Christopher.

"Whose?" said dream-Liz.

"Mine," said dream-Christopher.

When Christopher woke up, he still had that strange feeling of separation, like one thought was

over *here*, singing,	over *here*, singing
while another thought was	a different song.

This wasn't a completely new feeling—he'd had really bad headaches, and several mystery illnesses, during the past year. His disposition had changed recently, too. Some mornings, he'd wake up in his new apartment—which he'd moved into the previous fall—and have trouble getting out of bed; his thoughts couldn't convince his arms and legs to move. The commute from this new place to work was tough, and sometimes, while sitting in traffic in his Echo, Christopher would start punching the steering wheel as hard as he could. He didn't like talking to people, seeing people. His boss at the Department of Fiction—where he worked with a large team, writing and publishing official Coolidge narratives—had reprimanded Christopher several times for closing himself in his office. "The copy room is supposed to be an open space, so people can float through it," Janet had told him. "And a closed door—"

"I can't stand all the fucking *chatter*, Jan," Christopher groaned.

"A closed door sends the wrong message, is what I'm saying."

Christopher's headache worsened throughout the day. He kept running back to the bathroom to look in the mirror, and each time he did the shape in his forehead was more pronounced.

By mid-afternoon he could clearly see the sharp, bumpy edges of bricks and even a recessed mortar joint. Finally, the pain got so intense that he collapsed on the bathroom floor, started breathing hard, and occasionally screaming out. Then, all at once, water spilled from his forehead, and then blood, and then the wall emerged, jutting out of Christopher's eyes and creating a weird shadow on the back of his neck. Christopher's thoughts panicked and started shouting at each other over the wall—to call an ambulance or call Liz. But then Christopher remembered what she'd said that morning, that maybe this was anxiety or something temporary. Eventually he picked himself up, cleaned up the blood and fluid on the bathroom floor, and made himself a frozen burrito. In his mind, one thought calmed the others. "We're going to sleep on it and see how we're doing tomorrow, OK?" it announced.

By bedtime that night, though, the gray cement wall extended almost a foot away from his face—the wall felt so heavy as Christopher brushed his teeth that he could hardly hold his head up straight. He fell into bed but couldn't sleep— all night long, lost and displaced thoughts shouted to one another over the wall. "Clark?" hollered a thought in the right side of his brain. "Are you OK?"

"Rhonda!" shouted a thought in the left side. "Honey?"

The next day the wall was still there—it had grown bigger, in fact—so Christopher decided it was only prudent to get it checked out. He called his doctor and made an appointment for that afternoon, and then he showered and drove downtown— which was no easy feat, given the new blind spot in the center of his field of vision. He was standing at an intersection a few blocks from the doctor's office, though, when a bus passed by him and he noticed something strange: the cologne advertisement on the side of the bus showed a man with a tiny wall on his knee.

Christopher watched the bus fade away. Then the walk light illuminated and everyone started crossing the intersection. But Christopher didn't move. "You can walk," said a right-thought.

"Hold on a second," said a left-thought.

"Go! Walk!" said another thought.

"Did anyone see that bus?" said a left-thought.

"What bus?" said a right-thought.

"I saw it," said another right-thought. "So what?"

"So *what*? That guy on the side had a *wall*!"

Christopher stood on the corner for a minute, listening to the argument in his mind. Then he spun on his heels, walked back to his car, and drove to work. When he stepped into the copy room, he braced himself for a snide comment; no one said anything to him, though. Christopher sat down at his computer, took a picture of himself with the wall, and emailed it to Liz. *Cool or no?* Christopher wrote. *Would you date a guy who looked like this? Scratch that—forget I asked. But would you?* Then he hit send. Liz didn't reply, but when his assistant Danielle stopped by his office that afternoon to deliver a character study she said, "Hey—I really like your wall."

"Thank you," he said.

"I'm thinking of getting one," she said.

Christopher didn't know what that meant. "You should," he said.

· ✦ ·

Within a few weeks, Bodywalls were all the rage; you'd see ads for them in the fashion magazines and in commercials on TV, and people who weren't already growing them organically started having them surgically installed: cheekwalls, neckwalls, eyewalls. All of Coolidge's celebrities had them: Trox Dillon, October Wire, the Noun. Some people had more than one; Dillon had three really cool walls running over his forearm, each of them made from locally-sourced cement and graffitied by a different well-known street artist.

Christopher followed the trend, too, installing as many walls as he could afford. Over the following two months he added a total of *eleven* new walls: five in his face, four in his heart, one on his right forearm, one on his lower back. This involved a certain amount of risk, sure (whenever he visited Sammy's House of Walls on Inquiry Ave, they made him sign a legal form acknowledging the Surgeon General's warnings on the connections between walling and division), but didn't everything? Plus, the walls had changed Christopher's life for the better. His head was clearer now, and he wasn't so angry or cantankerous. He was calmer, and more productive, too.

Not only that, he liked the way the walls looked. Christopher wasn't particularly handsome—he was bald and overweight, and he wore thick glasses—but the walls sharpened his features, made him look almost tough. He'd gotten more dates recently, too, and even had to break up with a woman after things got weird in the bedroom; she was just far less interested in Christopher as a person than she was in his walls.

Christopher's progress was derailed that August, though, when he ran into Liz at a wedding. He should have expected to see her there—the bride was their former neighbor, after all—

but he hadn't spoken to her in a few weeks and didn't know if she'd been invited. Then he walked into the ballroom and saw Liz dancing with some *dude*—smoky eyes, thick beard—and the left side of Christopher's mind went crazy; his thoughts started screaming and kicking over mental furniture and lighting mind-fires and he couldn't calm them down. When Liz fell into Beardy's arms at the end of the song, Christopher stormed across the ballroom and shoved the guy good. By the way Beardy fell back and quickly regained his balance, though, Christopher knew the guy could kick his ass. Before the situation escalated, Liz took Christopher by the arm and led him out of the ballroom and into the hallway. "Have you lost your fucking mind?" she said.

"Who is that?" Christopher demanded.

"He's a brown belt in karate, is who he is," said Liz.

"What's his *name*?"

"Why does that matter?" Then Liz stepped back and seemed to notice Christopher's new bodywalls for the first time. "What are all these—things—in your face?" she said. "Don't you know what can happen, Chris?"

Christopher felt like he might cry. "Who *is* that guy, Liz?"

Liz fumed. "Look—I don't mind you calling me from time to time, or an occasional email. But you and are I not together anymore, Chris. Do you understand?"

When she said those words—"not" and "together" and "anymore"—Christopher felt a weird, wide pang in the middle of his body. He immediately knew what that meant—he remembered the brochures on halving at Sammy's—and he tried to stop it by wrapping his arms around himself in a frantic self-hug. "Are you alright?" Liz said. But Christopher didn't answer; he broke away from her and bolted down the hall and out to the parking lot, where he looked around desperately for some rope or thick tape. The closest thing he could find was some bungee cords in the back of a pickup truck. He grabbed them and wrapped them around himself, and then he ran to his car and tried to drive to the hospital. On his way there, though, his piece-of-shit Echo stalled out at a light, and when he got out to check the engine one of the bungee cords caught on the door and snapped. Christopher felt a sudden shift in body heat and a breeze blowing between his eyes as his two sides slipped apart, each one taking part of the wall with it. His right half reached for his left half—"Wait!" the right half of Christopher called—but the left half of him hopped across the street, hailed a taxi, and disappeared.

When the right half of Christopher woke up the next morning, he reached over to touch the wall that had severed him and checked to see that he was still only a half. He was, and overnight his centerwall had thickened. He hopped over to his laptop and Googled "walling" and "division." He found countless articles about the connections between the two, many of which appeared on a website called wallhelp.org. "Wallers need to watch for the following symptoms: scattered thoughts, inner turmoil, and headaches," the website read, and then, farther down the page, "There's currently no cure for wall-related divisions."

Christopher lived as a half for a while, and thus, was of two minds. The left half of him went underground, and later surfaced living out of a van down by the Coast of If. The right half of him, meanwhile, remained in the apartment they'd shared and stayed on at the DOF. Christopher's left half was content on his own—he had one-night and short-term connections, often with other walled halves and wild split personalities—but the right half of him was lonely and soon started looking to reconnect.

There were all sorts of ways to connect with people, or halves of people, at the time. At first, the right half of Christopher hoped to meet another half—a better half, even—on his own. When he didn't, he signed up for an online service—halfaconnection.com—and was soon digitally matched with someone.

The first person the service connected with the right half of Christopher was an old woman, Mrs. Limit, who did not speak English—she spoke a strange language that Christopher couldn't place and never learned (English Two, maybe, or Blixalese). Joined at the mind as they were, though, the right half of Christopher understood her suffering. Even with the wall dividing their thoughts, her mind shared memories of the first Bird War; her mourning for her husband, who died in Bird War II; her fleeing the village during the Great Nesting in Bird War IV. While the two halves' thoughts mostly agreed, though, there were occasional thoughtflicts. Mrs. Limit was a vegetarian and she followed a strict diet; Christopher would regularly eat FatBurgers and entire bags of chips. Mrs. Limit was truly kind and good—always thinking of others—and Christopher found that fucking annoying sometimes. When his assistant Danielle's husband was diagnosed with chronic forgetting, Mrs. Limit spent days discussing ways to help him: a fund drive, a benefit, a website. "Will you all *shut up*?" Christopher's thoughts finally shouted over the wall. "We don't even know this guy!"

Two years into the connection, though, poor Mrs. Limit died. Christopher was at the dentist machine's office when it happened; her half-heart stopped right there in the waiting room, and the right half of Christopher felt her separate from him and fall to the floor. Then the doctor machine's secretary-machine called Christopher in. "Oh," said the secretary-machine, staring down at the left half of the old woman crumpled on the ground.

Next, the right half of Christopher joined briefly with a traffic controller named Lou. But after three days of the halves' thoughts barking at each other over the wall in Christopher's mind, Lou disconnected from the right half of Christopher and said, "Hey. Listen. Bud."

"Yeah," said the right half of Christopher.

"This isn't—this just isn't," he said.

"No, I get it," said the right half of Christopher.

"I mean—"

"Sure," the right half of Christopher said. "I agree."

The right half of Christopher rented half an apartment on St. Pause Street, was promoted to Editor, and sent lonesome, rambling emails to Liz: *Are you even getting these? Please respond then! Do you know I have been thinking about sprucing up my kitchen. I want an island in the middle of it. Remember how we talked about having an island in our kitchen? I really like my new place. Not that you are asking. What about the kitchen that you have with your new family. Does it have an ISLAND? Do you not have time to read emails because you are so busy now with your new family? Do they know my name? Do they know that you were married to a man named Chris? I like it that you call me Chris. No one calls me that anymore.* When Liz cut off communication in a curt, threatening email that winter, Christopher resolved to stop looking for connections, and to try and find contentment as half a person.

One night after a Nots show at The Gallows the following June, the right half of Christopher walked back to his junky Echo and he couldn't get it started. He was leaning over the engine compartment, staring down into the mess of spirits and wires, when he heard a voice say, "You're still *driving* this piece of shit?"

The right half of Christopher turned to see the left half of Christopher standing beside him. The left half's hair was long, his centerwall was now spray-painted and his one arm was muscled. He looked tan, too, and the right half of Christopher noticed new wrinkles near his eyes. "It's the battery, I think," he said.

"Did you try jumping it?"

"I can't find—any cables," said the right half of Christopher.

"Hold on," said the left half of Christopher, and he trotted over to his halfcycle and came back with a pair of jumper cables. He attached them and the right half of Christopher turned the key. The Echo lulled and then turned over. "Awesome," said the right half of Christopher.

The left half removed the cables.

"Good show, hah?" said the right half.

"Fucking *awesome* show," said the left half. *Why won't anyone talk to me?*

"The Nots are still a very skilled band."

The left half chuckled. "Yes," he said in a mock British accent, "by George I think they are."

"Shut up," said the right half of Christopher.

"Good to see you," said the left half of Christopher, slapping the side of the vehicle. Then he walked off through the parking lot.

The right half of Christopher drove home that night thinking about his other half. It *was* good to see him, and he wished they'd had more time to talk. He thought of calling him the next day, but then realized he didn't know the left half's new number.

Lo and behold, though, the right half of Christopher saw his other half again a few weeks later while standing in line at Coffee or Else on Ginger Street. At first the right half didn't recognize his other half—all he saw was a wall that looked somewhat familiar—but then the left half shifted and the right half saw his half-face clearly. The right half of Christopher waited for his order—coffee with one sugar and half-and-half—and then went over to say hello. The left half looked up from the book he was reading, kicked out a chair, and said, "Have a seat."

The right half of Christopher sat.

"How's that car?" the left half asked.

"Awful," said the right half of Christopher. "I need a transformer. Can't *get* a transformer."

"You can in Coolidge Heights," said the left half.

"Yeah, on the black market," said the right half of Christopher. "That's *illegal.*"

The left half smiled. "So," he said.

The right half of Christopher shook off the idea. "What are you reading?"

The left half held up his book and the hair on the back of the right half of Christopher's neck stood up. "That's antifiction," he hissed.

"No shit," said the left half, and then, "How about you—you working?"

"Yes."

"Same job?" asked the left half.

"I'm an Editor now," said the right half of Christopher.

"Writing propaganda." The left half smiled. "A rat in the maze."

"Not at all," said the right half of Christopher. "I am a valuable commodity at one of Coolidge's most important—" The left half's half-smile took on a shit-eating quality that made the right half stop talking. "Anyway," he said.

The left half checked his watch and stood up. "I gotta run," he said. Then he squinted in the sunlight and looked up at the right half of Christopher. "You want to come with me?"

The right half of Christopher felt a rush of joy and fear. "Sure," he said, trying to sound nonchalant.

The left half led him out to his halfcycle and they drove away from the café, out past the Cages, and down to the left half's trailer by the sea. Then the left half led the right half out to the beach and they sat down in the sand. "Nice, huh?" said the left half.

The right half of Christopher looked out at the water. There was something strange about the clouds—they appeared to have *expressions*. "Do you see that?" he said.

"See what?" said the left half of Christopher.

"Those clouds out there?"

"What about them?"

"They're *looking* at us," the right half said.

"They're just clouds," said the left half. "You're too wound up. Just let the if free your mind."

"Easier said than done," said the right half.

"Shh," said the left half, sidling up next to him. "Shut up."

"What are you doing?" said the right half of Christopher.

"Stop talking, I said."

The right half of Christopher went silent. His wall ached for its counterpart.

"Now move closer to me," said the left half.

"We're already sitting very close," said the right half of Christopher.

"Closer," said the left half, softly.

The right half of Christopher moved closer, and the left half moved closer, and suddenly the two walls between them were connected. They fit together now like two pieces of a puzzle. And it was breathtaking/breathgiving—immediately, both halves had more oxygen in their lungs, more blood in their veins, more thoughts in their mind. Christopher's feet touched and his hands held each other, and he closed his eyes and lay back in the sand.

When the right half of Christopher woke up on the beach the next morning, the left half was nowhere to be found— neither on the shore nor in his trailer. The right half of Christopher found his shoe, called a cab and made his way back to his apartment.

Two nights later, though, the right half of Christopher was at home, reading a pamphlet, when he got a text from the left half. *U busy?* it said.

Wasn't sure I'd hear from you, the right half of Christopher replied.

What r u doing right now

Nada, the right half of Christopher wrote.

Can I come over?

The left half appeared at the right half of Christopher's apartment about a half an hour later. The right half of Christopher opened the door and pulled the left half into the living room, and the two halves pressed against each other hard.

Christopher's halves stayed connected the entire night. They didn't disconnect the next morning, either, or all the next day. They were still connected three days later, and two days after that. Soon they'd been reconnected for a full week.

Which isn't to say that Christopher's thoughts always got along. The wall in his mind remained, and the two halves bickered constantly. His right-thoughts were very organized, and spent all their time making mental to-do lists, but sometimes his left-thoughts just wouldn't feel like going anywhere or doing anything. When a right-thought chided him for being late, the left-thought said, "I would just love it if you'd be quiet for ten seconds."

"I've never known anyone so lazy," said the right-thought.

"I've never known anyone so lazy," mimicked the left-thought in a high-pitched voice.

"Guys," said a thought standing near the center of Christopher's mind.

"No, fuck him," said the right-thought. "He's always making fun of me and I'm *sick* of it."

"Just lay *off* why don't you," said the left-thought. "Seriously," he told the moderating thought, "if he doesn't shut up about his fucking *to-do* list I'm going to kill myself."

"Hold on a second," said the moderating thought.

"If he doesn't get on board and *do* something, I'm going to kill *myself*," said the right-thought.

"Can we just agree on some things?" said the moderator.

"I'll agree that he's a fucking asshole," said the left-thought.

"See? He's completely disrespectful!" said the right-thought.

"Can we all just admit," said the moderator, "that we're lonely?"

Neither thought said anything for a second. Then a right-thought said, "That's true."

The moderator said, "And that we've always *been* lonely?"

Thoughts on both sides of the wall nodded.

"And scared?" said the moderator.

"Yes," said another right-thought.

"Scared to lose anyone else," said a left-thought.

"Kind of scared for what's next," said the first right-thought.

"And sad," said another left-thought. "Aren't we super sad?"

When the thought said that word—"sad"—Christopher felt something crumble. A brick fell from the wall in his mind, and then another, and then another, until big sections of brick started toppling away. The two sides of thoughts walked toward the broken wall, and one or two thoughts tentatively stepped over it, and before Christopher knew what was happening right-thoughts were hugging left-thoughts, and left-thoughts were weeping on the shoulders of right-thoughts, and hallelujah, for the first time in as long as he could remember, at least for a brief moment, Christopher felt whole.

SUCCESS STORY

We were driving through Geryk Falls when I saw the flash of success on the side of the road and I told my wife—I was still married at the time—to stop the car. "Why?" she said. "I just saw some success on the side of the road!" I hollered. Liz made a face. "Pull over!" I shouted.

She stopped the car and I got out and ran—limped—as fast as I could back to the spot where I'd seen the success. Sure enough, there it was: a shiny success half-buried in the leaves. I picked it up and brushed it off. I'll admit that it was a bit outdated—made mostly of earning a lot of money, buying a big gaudy house, that sort of thing—but still, I thought it might be worth something.

"Oh Chris," my wife said, stepping up behind me. "It's ancient!"

"Even so," I said.

"Look," she said, "it's covered with bugs." And just as she said that, I noticed the tiny somethings crawling out from a hole in the wet successful wood. "Ack," I said, and flung the thing to the ground. Then I limped back to the car and we drove away. I never saw that success again—or any success for that matter. I continued to fail—to fail better, and better still. I failed as a writer, as a friend, as a husband, as an ex-husband, as a bookstore owner, as a bookstore employee, as a clord, as a writer, as a gutter installer, as a prayor, as an HVAC technician, as a landlord, as a waste disposal associate, as a moderate eater, as a moderate drinker, as an auto mechanic, as a coffee drinker, as a tea drinker, as a sitter, as a stander, as a breather. Eventually, I was one of the best failers in western Massachusetts. Then I began failing strongly at the state level, and eventually in national competitions. By the fall of 2013 I was ranked number one. I even appeared on the Flip Dapple show! "Let me give you a test," said Dapple. "OK," I said. "What is the capital of California?" I peed myself. "Wow," said Dapple, and he stood up and clapped.

The following spring, though, I started hearing rumors about a woman in Vancouver named Laura DeNox who was failing in new ways that no one had ever seen before. I saw videos of her on YouTube—one of her failing to eat, another of her not even able to get up in the morning—and her name was all over Twitter: "She might seriously be the best failure in the history of trying," tweeted @socoool. Someone named @buley responded "No way! Chris Boucher is the best failure since Rhonda O'Dial." "Boucher's a has-been," @socoool responded.

I'll be honest—I was scared of DeNox. Try as I might to avoid a fail-off with her, though, I could not. I trained with world-renowned failer Corduroy Oll for six months before the event. Corduroy had me failing around the clock: failing to tie my shoes, even, and to brush my teeth. Maybe you tuned into ESPN for the competition and saw how I looked when I arrived in Houston: fat, unshaven, wearing two different shoes. That was all Corduroy's influence.

Like all fail-offs, the challenges were broken down into categories. For the Workplace challenge, they drove us to an office building filled with cameras and broadcast the results live. DeNox found a faux supply closet on set and managed to mistakenly lock herself inside it: a pretty good fuckup, all told. I countered, though, by sending an incredibly personal and embarrassing email to the whole office instead of to the one person I'd written it for, which resulted in immediate termination and the loss of a good friend.

Then we had to fail at Street Smarts. They drove us out to a dangerous street and a man approached me and asked me for money. I didn't have any, so I offered him my wedding ring.

"All I need is a dollar, hombre," he said.

"Take it, take it," I said, dropping the ring into his open palm. "It belonged to my father."

The crowd, assembled behind a railing across the street, oohed and clapped.

But DeNox one-upped me. When the same actor asked her for money, she kissed him on the mouth and gave him her social security card, which he immediately sold to some hackers who stole her identity. The crowd went wild.

The third and final leg of the fail-off was Marital. Our spouses took the stage in front of an audience and we stood opposite them. DeNox squared her shoulders toward her husband, shrugged, and said, "I'm sorry, honey. But I just don't find you very interesting anymore."

In retrospect, this was DeNox's critical error. See, you can't just not try—that's not a fail. The secret to failing is trying your ass off. I'd been trying and failing to tell Liz how I felt for years—I could do it again no problem. I walked up to her where she stood and said, "Honey? I am the spoon and you are the fork."

My wife's face contorted. "What does that even mean?"

The crowd began to chant: "Fail! Fail!"

"I," I said. "I am a tree and you are a cloud."

"What are you saying?" Liz said. "That I'm fat?"

"Fail! Fail! Fail!"

"You are a virus and I am the same virus!" I shouted.

"Gross, Chris!" my wife said. "What is the matter with you?" Then she stormed off the stage; I didn't see her again for months. The crowd cheered for me and the host ushered DeNox into the wings. Then he placed a glass trophy in my hands and I tried to lift it over my head. It was too heavy, though; I fumbled it and it fell to the floor and shattered. When I bent down to gather the shards, I sliced my finger on a piece of glass. I held up my bloody hand, and the crowd erupted and sprang to their feet.

Can anyone hear me? Is anyone out there?

CALL AND RESPONSE

That was the winter I gave up writing and prayed. Professionally, I mean—I was lucky enough to get a job in Coolidge's City Hall, where I worked the prayer switchboard. At the time, I was living with Liz in a one-room underground flat—the "coffins," they called these apartments—with Liz's parents, her sister Marie, and Marie's two sons. That was a bad chapter for Coolidge: The war with Blix was very loud, and resources no more than a murmur. Our electricity was unreliable, and our phones stopped working altogether. We ate mostly paste, drank mostly sorrow. Even so, though, we had more than most other towns. The border to Blix was closed, and Blixers tried every way imaginable to get across. In Coolidge, meanwhile, they were evicting people every day: the very tall, for example, and then the very short, and then the especially nervous, and then anyone who laughed. All this resulted in a flood of prayers. Those outside Coolidge prayed to be let in; those living in Coolidge prayed to stay.

Most nights, Liz worked the night shift at the hospital. Then she'd come home, make me a paste sandwich, and hug me on my way out the door. I'd leave home and ride the train through the subtext to the city center. In those days, the trains were erratic, dimly lit, and extremely violent. The rule of thumb in the subtext was: If you see something, say nothing. I saw one or two fights on the train per day, and I'd seen four people killed. My third week riding the train, I saw someone hanged in the next car over. I pulled my knees closer as the body swayed to the jolt of the train. *Say nothing,* I told myself. *Tell no one.* And that's what I did.

City Hall was different: It was beautiful. All the rooms were bright and warm, and you could use the bathroom down the hall whenever you needed to. My first day, I reported to Seat 9929 in Switchroom 2264667 and my boss, a man named Stevens, sat down next to me to show me the terminal. "Stevens," he said, extending his hand.

"Chris," I said.

"Chris—fantastic," Stevens said. "Good to meet you. You know anything about prayers?"

"A little," I said.

"You pray personally?"

"Sometimes," I said.

"To whom?"

"To my girlfriend, mostly. When we were first dating, we used to pray poems—"

"So you know prayers can take physical shape. That they have weight, mass."

"Sure," I said.

"Well, the prayers you're talking about—person-to-persons—are small, the size of books or basketballs. The ones we get here, at City Hall? They can be as big as refrigerators. Cars. I once picked up a prayer as big as a rhino."

"Wow," I said.

"And we get a ton of 'em," said Stevens.

"Can I ask what the prayers are *for*?"

Stevens leaned over on his knees. "Listen, Chris," he said. "Soon the stories in Coolidge will be fantastic again. Right?"

"Absolutely," I said.

"But right now they're not so great; we're still in a pre-fantastic time. So people pray to City Hall for better stories, things we can't give 'em: stories of food, stories of jobs, all sorts of shit. And these prayers are a problem for the admins. One," he said, holding up one finger, "they introduce a lot of whining and negativity. Two, they cause damage! They fuck up the paint, dent the siding! And we can't have that, can we?"

"No sir," I said.

"So this," he said, sweeping his hand, "is our prayer filtration system."

I looked around the giant room. There must have been 500 terminals, each of them manned with someone wearing headphones and staring at a screen.

"These terminals pick up the prayers, scan them, and either accept them—" he showed me the keypad, the buttons that read "accept" and "kill," "—or kill them before they hit us."

I looked to the terminal next to me, where a woman with a shaved head and a tattoo of hair kept clicking the "kill" button. "Fuck you," she was whispering, "and you, and you, and you."

"Ready to give it a go?" said Stevens.

I nodded and we both put on headphones. Then Stevens clicked on my terminal. I heard two or three prayers simultaneously, until Stevens turned a dial to isolate one. *—elp,* it said, *they're saying I have to leave Coolidge but I CAN'T, you don't know what I've been through—*

"See, now that's very negative," said Stevens. "Kill it."

I killed it.

Stevens clapped me on the shoulder and twisted the dial to find another prayer: *What I want to know is—tak—does the Statue of Coolidge hate me? Or people like me?* Then the prayor started speaking in another language.

"Wah," Stevens mock-whined. "Also—she's not praying in American. Kill."

I killed it and picked up a third prayer. *Great Statue of Coolidge*, it began. *I just want to say how grateful I am for your wisdom, and your strength, and for taking zero shit from the whiners and losers out there that—*

"Ah, now see? That's very nice. Very sweet. Accept."

I worked my ass off at that job. Even though there were thousands of operators like me in those rooms, I usually worked nine or ten hours straight without taking a break. There were just so many prayers! And despite our best efforts, downtrodden psalms would still slip through every now and again; we'd hear them ding the side of the building or see them glance off the window. "Fuck!" Stevens would shout. "Focus, people!"

I worked the prayer switchboard for three months—the same three months that Coolidge walled itself off from Geryk and West Geryk. During that time prayer volume increased twofold. Which, from my perspective, was good—it meant more dollars for food and coffin-rent.

Back home, though, everyone was worried—people we knew were disappearing or sick and in need of help. By March most of the stores were cleaned out, and it became more and more difficult to find staples like sandwich paste and toilet paper.

One night over dinner, Liz's nephew Gerald took a bite out of his paste sandwich and said, "Hey Chris. What's the—" But the word was muffled—it sounded like "olm."

"Finish chewing," Marie told him.

He did so and said, "Swarm. What's the swarm?"

"The what?" I said.

"These sandwiches are delicious," said Liz's mother.

"I toasted the paste is why," said Liz.

"The swarm," said Gerald.

"*Swarm*? I don't know *what* that is," I said.

Gerald looked confused. "Frank at school said—"

"Frank's a dumbass," said Gerald's brother Bruce.

"Language, Brucey!" said Marie.

"But he is," said Bruce.

"Not in this coffin he isn't, Bruce," I said. "Frank is pre-fantastic now, but soon he will be amazing. Right?"

Bruce shrugged.

"Anyway, he keeps talking about a swarm," Gerald told his sandwich.

The next day began like any other. I went into work, filtered as many prayers as I could, and tried to ignore Amanda, the tattooed hair woman, who made explosion noises—*bchoo! bchoo!*—every time she killed a prayer.

But then something happened. All of a sudden, my terminal went berserk—instead of six or seven prayers, it showed: *all* prayers. Thousands, maybe more. Amanda sat up—her screen showed the same. Everyone began shouting. Then we felt a jolt on the far wall, and I saw a psalm smack against the window.

"What the fuck, people!" shouted Stevens.

"It's an attack," Amanda said quietly.

Another prayer hit us—so hard this time that a wall caved in—and an alarm sounded. Stevens's face went white and he started sprinting down the aisle. "Nets!" he shouted, and through the window I saw giant nets raise up around City Hall.

Meanwhile, I tried to kill as many prayers as I could: *I am going to freeze out here—* and, *I would rather die than live like this—* and, *I am a PERSON of VALUE. Do you hear me?* But it wasn't enough—soon I heard the sound of ripping as the prayers cut through the nets, and then our terminal screens went dark and the lights went out. People started screaming and running in every direction. Then the ceiling collapsed across the room and *Everyone deserves happiness!* crashed through a window and crushed four operators.

"No!" shouted Stevens, but then he was hit in the stomach by *Love wins.*

I threw off my headphones and crouched under my desk. *Liz,* I prayed.

Hey! my wife prayed back. *Surprised to hear from you in the middle of the—*

I'm in deep trouble here, I prayed. *I don't know—*

Where—on the train?

At work, I said. *We're under some sort of attack.*

What? she prayed. *Is it Blix, or—*

A prayer the size of a Volkswagen hurtled through the wall to my right.

I don't know, I prayed to her. *Listen—if I don't make it back—*

What? What do you mean?

If I don't—

What? she prayed. *No no. Chris. Please.* Tears came through the prayer. *I want to grow old with you in this coffin.*

We demand a new, more compassionate—fell through the drop ceiling and Amanda howled in pain.

I prayed, *Tell everyone*—

WE ARE ALL CONNECTED! DO YOU NOT SEE THAT WE ARE ALL CONNECTED? crashed down on my desk.

I can't tell you how I made it out of there. Almost every operator up there that day died. But an emergency worker—6822135e, his name was—carried me out. I woke up in a hospital. Why me? I was ready for my story to end right there in City Hall.

Tell everyone it's OK, I prayed from under the desk. *That I love them and always will. That I was SURROUNDED by hope and love.* And then the prayers came through the ceiling, hundreds of them, louder and brighter and more beautiful than anything I'd ever seen, and the last thing I remember was their weight on top of me.

HOW TO GET RID OF A CHRISTOPHER BOUCHER

It's not easy to do. Bouchers are nags! If a Boucher shows up at your door, which they do often, start by saying, "Shoo!" or "Git!" If that doesn't deter the Boucher—if he starts to cry or just stands there—shout "No one loves you!" If you're lucky, he'll limp off into the woods.

If verbal abuse alone doesn't work, you'll have to be more forceful. You might have to beat the Boucher with a stick. Don't *have* a stick? Go to getridofboucher.com. There you'll find a product called the **BoucherBat**, which is sculpted exactly the right size to cause the most damage to Boucher's skull. Hit him once in the head and once in the groin. Alternatively, you might opt for a **Boucher Taser**, which shocks Boucher with memories. Finally, you might consider **Boucher Detectors**, which come armed with a **Truth Alarm**. If Boucher steps onto your property, the Detectors tell him the Truth: that he is alone and always will be. Your Boucher will undoubtedly cover his ears and turn and run from that Truth as fast as he can.

Unless, that is, Boucher is wearing Truth-Blocking headphones. In that case, call **The Mothers** (1-888-MOTHERS) and report the Boucher on your premises. The Mothers will swoop in, capture the Boucher and send him for re-training: he'll emerge a Morkan or an O'Malley.

BOUCHER Q & A

How do I know if there's a Boucher nearby?

Even if you don't have Boucher Detectors installed, you can usually smell a Boucher from as far as fifty yards away. Most Bouchers have a distinct odor, a mix of sweat and urine. Also, listen for the sound of crying. Bouchers cry at least five times a day.

Why does my Boucher have a hole in his chest?

See "The Unloveables."

What if I'm married to a Christopher Boucher?

Divorce him immediately! If you're in Coolidge, you can stop by one of those new drive-thru divorce kiosks—I believe most other states have them now, too. Get to one fast and click "Insta-Divorce." Under that menu there's an option to "Divorce a Christopher Boucher." Click that. And don't worry for a minute about the divorce's effect on Boucher; most Bouchers don't have hearts.

What's so bad about Christopher Bouchers in the first place? Why are they so difficult to be around?

Who do you think is causing all of this? It's Boucher who invented the bodywalls, conceived of the Lipolian, assembled the Unloveables, erected the Tetherly, imagined a Suicide, and put his own big dumb fucking head in the sky. It's Boucher who killed Bellis, who killed the Narrator as well. And this is our revenge. He'll find no safe quarter, not one ounce of happiness—not in writing, or with Liz, or at the Tetherly, or anywhere else. No one here loves him; no one ever will.

I know that it can be unnerving to wake up one morning and find a Christopher Boucher in your life. By following the steps listed above, though, you can make that Boucher someone else's problem and return to a life that is serene, productive, and Boucher-free.

BEAUTIFUL OUTLAW

To know the story of The Lipolian you're going to have to go back with me all the way—back to those days of my childhood when I worked with my dad, the best setman in the Pioneer Valley. And I was his assistant his was I and. For years, I worked on some of the trillest books published. Have you read *Tarmac*, by Trox Dillon? My father built the gravesite in that first scene. The house with the tree that runs up through the floor in Lurie Less's *American Fowl*? We crafted that tree out of fiberglass and foam. Or the open-mouth moment in Core Allen's *Lava Lamp*? I carved those teeth! I can still remember my dad yelling at me about it from across the page. "Hey, _____!"

"Yeah!" I shouted back.

"Which tooth are you on?"

"I'm three teeth in," I said.

"Are you kidding me? You should be done by now!"

"Everything OK?" said Allen, pacing on the surface of the page.

"It's not the fuckin' Mona Lisa," my dad hollered. "It's one scene!"

We weren't a big shop, like Bergen Sets in New York, which has a forty-person crew, or Backgrounds Ltd, which, Jesus, employs a hundred or more people internationally. But we were respected by the big houses for our reliability and consistent product. I was a pretty good scenic painter, and a passable draughtsman too, and I don't mind telling you that I had numerous standing offers—one from Neitherton, another from Achoo! Books—to work as an in-house setman.

My father was the real talent, though—a visionary when it came to sets for short stories, novels, and the occasional memoir. Sometimes he was so gil that he was almost more of a co-author. I can still remember my dad's late-night meetings inside the novels of those authors who were blocked or couldn't find the next scene—how my dad would stand on the blank page with them and dance from corner to corner, trying to explain where a certain building could stand or how the characters might move through the space. Bill Toom told me he never would have written *Cold Eye* were it not for my father, and Kim Meridian once dropped my dad's name in an interview. "Far as sets go," Meridian said, "I believe Bellis _____ has the best eye in the business."

My father was killed in 2012 when he fell from a set while working on an experimental novel called *Golden Delicious*. He was inside the book-in-progress, standing on some scaffolding and painting trees, when the scaffolding buckled and collapsed. I was on the ground, maybe fifty feet away, and I felt the ground rumble. I looked up to see my dad reach for a tree branch, and then for the scaffolding, finding nothing and falling forty feet or so. He landed on the page and died upon impact.

His death could have been avoided had the author, Chris Boucher, not broken a cardinal rule of storywork. The author is never, *ever*, supposed to be writing while the crew is onsite—every booker in America knows that. In the statement that

Boucher gave to the traffic cones afterward, he said he *hadn't* been writing—that he'd had a sudden "epiphany." The pages themselves, he realized, could be porous, full of holes. He wrote down the idea—"Just to remember it," he said—in the margin. As soon as the idea took hold in the fibers, though, the page destabilized, the first holes appeared, and the scaffolding faltered.

We buried my dad on his favorite page, in a spot where he used to like to watch the sun set. The next day, I hired the sharkiest suits I could find to go after Boucher. I wanted to stare that booker down in a courtroom, have a gavel take writing from him forever.

When he heard about the suits, Boucher wrote me a letter. *Please, _____, he wrote. Writing is ALL I HAVE. I know you're pissed at me but I am working on something now that I think could really break it open—about fear, and love, and LOSS. Remember we even sketched out the sets? I want to incorporate those, in honor of your dad.*

I don't know if you heard, but Liz and I broke up again. She says it's for good this time. It's a really tough time for me—for you too, I know—so I'm asking you, out of the goodness of your heart—

And so on. Two days before the scheduled start of the trial, we settled: Boucher agreed to give up writing for one year if I called off the suits. Boucher's laptop, notebooks, and pens were confiscated—he couldn't even write checks. If he was found with so much as a shopping list, we agreed, the suits would reopen the case. In fact, I heard Boucher gave up books altogether—that he took a job fixing gutters with Bill Sunflower.

I remember my ex-fiancée asking me, weeks before we separated, if all of this made me feel better. And it did! Boucher had hurt people. Every time he had an idea or wished he could write a story, I wanted him to think of my father, remember how his blood spilled across the white paper.

In the months following the settlement, I tried to put my life back together. I couldn't go back to working in sets—I rejected stories altogether, in fact—so I took on some renovation jobs: a barn in Williamsburg, a demo in Goshen, some others. Then I heard that Gar Bell, an exterminator I knew in Florence, was looking for a part-time poemcatcher. I stopped by the shop to tell him I was interested and he hired me on the spot. It was a pretty straightforward transition: After all those years in stories, I knew where poems hid, the places they liked to burrow—I'd caught hundreds of them over the years. Sonnets in your belfry? No problem. Haiku chewing your wires? I'm your man.

I worked at Gar's for two years. His shop was a grimy shrug that smelled of words and solvents, but it was good, honest work—and there was plenty of it. We handled our share of outbreaks and infestations, but I spent most of my time driving Gar's orange van from page to page to visit our regular clients and spray for poems. By my second year at Gar's, I was actually pulling in a fair amount of money. I started to think I might start my own verse-extermination shop someday, maybe even a series of them.

Like I said, though: This was before the Lipolian—before the day that fall when I walked into the shop with two dead poems over my shoulder and saw a customer standing at the front desk. I knew who he was before he even turned around— I would have recognized his pitiful bald spot anywhere.

It was Chris Boucher.

I was so stunned to see him that I stopped in my tracks. The door clanged loudly behind me and Boucher turned around. He'd gotten fat and lost more hair.

"_____," said Gar, "this is an author, and he—"

"Out," I said. "Get out of my shop right now."

"Just wait a second," said Boucher cautiously. "Can I just—"

"Mr. Bowcher stopped by to see if—"

"It's boo-shay," said Boucher quietly.

"Did you hear what I said?" I stormed up to him. "Out. Right now."

"Will you just hear what I have to say?" Boucher said. "I need your help."

"Help!" I squawked. "What *kind* of help?"

See, I'd known Boucher my whole life—we'd once been good friends. In high school, I was one of his *only* friends—everyone else pitied him. Chris was raised by televisions, with no real family to speak of, and he was dumb and fragile. How many times did I look across the room to see Boucher crying at his desk? Whenever the teacher asked what was wrong, he'd say something strange—that the chalk had Alzheimer's, or that one of his thoughts was lost.

"Lost where?" Mr. Kirval asked.

"Starving in the wilderness," said Boucher.

"What *wilderness*?"

"In my mind," Boucher said.

Then Boucher started telling stories, rearranging his life on the page. He was always the shortest kid in the class, for example, but one day he arrived to school standing seven feet tall. Ms. McChair, the English teacher, gave him detention and scolded him until he shrunk back down to normal size. That same spring, we were playing baseball at Calvin Field when Corn Douglas hit a fly ball into right field; Boucher revised the mid-air ball into a hamburger, caught it, and took a bite. Coach Depression leapt off the bench and ran out to the field. "What the crap was that?" he said.

"I'm learning revision," said Boucher.

"Not here you aren't," said the coach. "Sit your ass down on that bench."

It was like that everywhere for Chris: he was a sorry, a whatfor. And when he wouldn't stop telling stories—changing the classroom into a junkyard, or the chalkboard into a crystal-clear window—the assistant principal put him in a room by himself. There wasn't even a teacher in there—it was just Chris and some wild, troublemaking paragraphs.

Eventually, Chris wrestled some of those paragraphs into a book. And for one reason or another—pity, I suppose—my father always rooted for Boucher; he wanted to help him out. When Boucher needed a set or props, my Dad always gave him the family discount. "He's not exactly the next Maude Crowne," dad told me once—meaning, he's not going to make us any real money—"but his heart's in the right place."

All this took place in my hometown of Coolidge, Massachusetts, a writers' town if there ever was one. Coolidge was probably the second- or third-most popular place in New England for letterbuilders and storytenants to live. Because it wasn't really close to anything, Coolidge was affordable enough for writers to rent out space for their novels or stories. You'd see these stories everywhere in Coolidge, just begging to be told. Walking into Attitude or the JavaNet, you'd often find yourself sitting next to a trope, a theme, or a character. Sometimes two verbs would be making out in the margin, or a novel would be playing saxophone on the stage. God, what I wouldn't give to get back there now.

For the seven or eight years that we were all working together, Boucher would write strange, elaborate sets for us to build—one featuring a talking Colorado; another about a man with a car attached to his abdomen—and we'd do our best to realize them. Most nights, when we all threw in the towel, the three of us would lock up the front cover of the book-in-progress and drive down to the Denouement—the best, cheapest bar on the page—where my father would regale Boucher with his best stories:

"And we had *no* time, and no meaning—"

"Shit," Boucher would say.

"So we took an old war that someone had in the back—"

"No," Boucher asked.

My father leaned forward on his stool. "And made that war into a bridge."

"Wow!" said Boucher.

Or:

"We can all see that the apology isn't there. And that it *needs* to be there for the next scene."

"You must have been *freaking* out."

"So Leo," my Dad said. "You know Leo Dueron?"

"Sure—sure."

"Leo jumps into a harness, drops down *from the rafter*, places the apology on the divan—"

"You are *kidding* me," said Boucher.

"And then we pull him up. Ten seconds before the scene starts."

I'd heard these stories a hundred times; I could have heard them a hundred more.

The Denouement was a character bar, so most of the people in the place were trying to drink away that day's plot. It wasn't strange for things to get out of hand—for a flag to start a fight with a metaphor, or a television and an octopus to suddenly grapple. When that happened, my dad would often step in and settle them down. Sometimes Boucher and I got involved as well. Once, a thriller caught Boucher staring at her and she knocked his drink out of his hand, and I stepped in to protect him. Another time, I fell into a dystopia by mistake coming back from the bathroom, and Boucher leapt between us.

Boucher had gone ahead and published *Golden Delicious*, the novel that killed my father, but it was halfhearted and clouded in controversy. After the settlement and all that bad press, I figured he'd never write again.

But now here he stood, his eyes late-night supermarkets. He seemed honestly afraid of me, and he should have been; I was nothing but anger those days. Other than Gar, I was all alone in the world. A year earlier, my fiancée had left me at the altar. I had a pet dog who, in the weeks before this, decided I was too depressing to be around and filed for a legal separation. These days I hardly went home—I spent most of my nights at Gar's, on a poem-infested cot. Which was maybe why I refrained from punching Boucher out or dragging him out the door. Instead I said, "Fine. You've got thirty seconds. Talk."

"OK," he stammered. "Here's the— it's— "

"Twenty-nine," I said. "Twenty-eight."

Boucher huffed. "I'm working on a new book."

"A *novel?*" I could barely say the word.

"There's nothing about you in there," he said, his voice quivering. "Just chapters about the floating heads, the language zoo, my bodywall, some other sorrows."

"Sounds like a hoot," I said.

"But I've got an infestation of some sort."

"Poems?" said Gar.

The author shook his head. "I don't know—I'm seeing some strange words on the page."

"Are there line breaks?" I said. "Is there any form to it?"

Boucher shook his head. "I don't think so. Your dad helped me with something like this once. There was some vegetation in the language—"

"It was a fungus," I said.

"—which he treated with something," said the author.

"It was basic verbal bacteria," I told Gar. "We just scrubbed the words with solvent."

"This is something else, then. I wouldn't bother you with it, but I don't have anyone else I can call. And I've got a whole crew waiting on this. At least twenty characters. An editor! A narrator. Sixteen different settings."

"Who's doing the sets?"

"Nehali," said the author.

"Christ," I spat.

"I've already called two other exterminators, but they were both too expensive."

"Does Joe know what you did? That you *killed* someone in your last book?"

"Of course he does," said Boucher. "Everyone knows."

I could feel Gar staring at me.

"Please, _____. I don't have anyone else I can ask."

I tried to find the words to make him leave—*Get out*, or *Fuck off*—but I couldn't say them. I just kept thinking of my father, who would want me to help Boucher.

"Please," said Boucher.

I crossed my arms. "I'll give you one hour," I said. "Just to take a look around and tell you what I see. And then I'm gone. OK?"

"That's great, _____," said Boucher. "Thanks. Thank you so much."

I tried not to think back on my days in novels, but sometimes I couldn't help it. I *was* born in a book, after all, and I spent my childhood in words: hiding under them, hopping from one to the next, stealing one now and again for fun. Books were my playground, and they still are. Most of my childhood friends were characters, or children of the bookers who worked with my father. Remember the talking star in *Finish Your Breakfast*? That star lived on the next page over from us for a year—I went to the Page 31 Middle School with her kids. Then my dad moved to another novel called *Cartilage!*, and I switched schools and became friends with new characters. I had friends in every style: In high school I hung out mainly with Ixentialists. In college I dated a Physicata.

I can't remember a time, either, when I wasn't working with my dad. I could route a page at twelve, paint a backdrop at fourteen, manage an entire *scene* by sixteen. I majored in set design in college and went to work with my dad soon afterward. From then on he and I were essentially partners.

Try as I might not to think about those days now, I'd occasionally catch myself going back to the sets we were most proud of—the Montreal facade in *Catapult*, the Mars scene in *The Living Room*. Or I'd go back to those moments *after* the stories, when our workday was done, all the characters gone home, the entire novel quiet. Like the night when, after six months of work, we finally finished the set for Annabel Trivulex's *Moontree*. My dad went out and brought back grinders and beers to the empty set, and we sat on the edge of the fake eddy, swigging beer and talking as the sun fell over the back of the page. "Look at that sunset," I said.

"And *you* built that sun," my dad said.

"Only the facade," I said. "You wired it."

"Still," he said. "That's good work. *Great* work, in fact." Then we finished our food, swept up the crumbs, turned off the novel's lights and closed the cover behind us.

The next morning I stepped into the book and walked out to the copyright page. Boucher was late as usual; by the time he arrived I'd checked the binding and tested the font and I was taking fiber and ink samples. "It's almost seven," I told him.

"Sorry," he said, tucking in his shirt.

I looked off into the distance. "Where we going?" I urred.

"Chapter Five," he said. "We'll take a train." He pointed across the page, to a staircase leading into the fiber.

"Listen," I said, planting my feet on the paper. "I don't want to go too far into the book."

"I know," Boucher said.

"Fifty pages max."

Boucher snapped his gum.

"I'm serious," I said. I knew Boucher—he was unorganized, easily distracted, terrible at planning. Back when we were friends, he was always running late, lost, a step behind. When we were growing up, how many times did Boucher lock himself out of his own house by mistake? And I could think of at least two incidents when we'd broken down because his car ran out of gas. "No problem," he said now. "Seriously. These are pretty short chapters, most of them."

I followed him down into the subtext, where we caught an inbound train. As I held the railing and we catapulted through the fictions, I looked around at the other characters on the train: a man wearing a tie-dyed shirt and a Quiet Riot bandana; an old rolltop desk muttering to itself; a woman with a leash tied around her own foot; a harp reading a book, and about a dozen others. Between stations, I saw bits of words—"ka," "ish"— flash by the windows, followed by scenes: a woman trudging down a country highway; a novel working in a field. "How much farther?" I hollered.

"Two more stops," Boucher shouted.

I gripped the overhead railing tighter. The subtext always made me anxious. My dad had warned me repeatedly to avoid it—had told me story after story about people getting lost under the page, in some sort of inference, and never making it back up to the surface. Once, he and I had to drop down into the page to fasten a set to the footer with screws, and I pretended I was falling—"Whoa! Whoa!"—until my Dad boomed at me to stop it. "Don't fuck around! People get killed down here like *that*," he said, snapping his fingers.

"Killed by what?" I asked, dumbly.

"By whim! Readers' thoughts! Or whatever strange, half-conceived characters live down here."

As I got older, I heard more rumors about the endless mysteries of the subtext—talk of four-dimensional spiders, falsepeople, pure themes, alligator halves, headless characters, dead symbols, wandering coffins, moaning mouths with no faces, nots, knots (and knotted nots!), raw ifs, the souls of sounds, suicides, corianders, plaxes, obs and do's, versionifications, wrongdeaths, half deaths, metadeaths, essences, signifiers without signs, signs without signifiers, lost symbols, dead motifs, the ghost of porta-potties, murdered themes, socksouls, origami that had come unfolded, lost rain, old notions, wandering cancers, ticks of storage, eddas and sturms, etceteras, et cetera.

"This is our stop," Boucher said, as the train slowed. We stepped out of the train and walked onto the platform, up the stairs and onto the page. I immediately recognized myself: I saw a storefront my father had designed, a happiness hydrant I'd helped build, a bookstore sign—"Tomorrow Books," it read—I'd painted myself. "You fucker," I said.

"What?" said Boucher.

These sets were my father's, preliminary construction for a third novel that Boucher was in the early stages of when my father fell. I'd assumed Boucher had thrown these sets away.

"This scenery," I said, pointing to the facades, "is not yours to use."

"OK—OK," Boucher stammered. "I thought Bellis would have *wanted* me to use it."

"You have Nehali pull these down or I walk right now."

"I will, OK? If that's what you want. Tomorrow morning, first thing."

I spat onto the page. "Show me the poems," I said.

Boucher led me across the street to the opposite page, where he stood me in the middle of the paragraph—a paragraph, as it were, about the death of the book's narrator. "I don't see any verse here at all," I said.

"OK, but take a look at this sentence," Boucher said, and he pointed to one that read "They drew an outpatient of his bodycheck on the pagoda."

"What about it?"

"Does that sentence look weird to you?"

I stared at it.

You were the love of my life.

"Because it's not the sentence I wrote," said Boucher.

"What do you mean?"

"I wrote 'They drew an outline of his body on the page.' But someone changed it."

"Who changed it?" I said.

"I have no idea," Boucher said.

I knelt down and studied the sentence, and something inside me sighed. Then I pulled the sentence off the page and picked it up.

"What are you doing?" said Boucher.

I threw the phrase over my shoulder. "I'm taking it back to the shop," I said.

"What for?" said Boucher.

"To see what it knows," I said. But even then I knew—I already knew what this was, where it had come from. I just needed to be sure.

· ✦ ·

Back at Gar's, I ran the sentence through the SCANson, by far the most advanced and expensive machine in our office. The SCANson's close readings were beyond compare; the machine could take one look at a sentence or phrase and give you its entire backstory—its origin, lineage, ink breakdown, et cetera, all listed on a dot-matrix printout.

Like I said, though, I pretty much knew what the SCANson would tell me. I anticipated a mid-twentieth-century signature, and that's what I saw. I suspected French origins, and I was correct. I anticipated constraints, and I saw them. While I didn't yet know how, I already thought this would lead back to my father in some way—that whatever was happening here had something to do with him.

The next morning, I drove over to Boucher's book and found him in the Table of Contents. I handed the sentence over to him and said, "You've got a Lipolian."

"A what?" he said.

"Lipolian," I said.

"What is that? A kind of poem?"

"Remember—the Lipolou? We discussed them in school. That French school of writers and mathematicians? Repec, Nequeu, all of them?"

Boucher stared at me dumbly.

"We spent a whole month on them. They're these writers who use all sorts of constraints. They'll only let themselves use certain letters, or write using words that *lack* a letter. Palindromes, anagrams, that sort of thing. They'll write a poem made up of lines from other poems, or one that spells a word out through its letters' absence—that's called a *belle absente*. This really doesn't ring a bell?"

Boucher stared at the dead sentence on the page. Standing there beside him, I tried to remember more about the Lipolou: how they worked, which books of theirs I'd read. My dad and I had worked with Lipolians a few times; once, when I was a kid, he designed the sets for a book by Brigitte Remillard, whose novel *c u b e* kept unfolding and unfolding—my dad always said that it was one of the most difficult sets he ever built.

Then it came to me. "I just remembered," I told Boucher. "This is called an 'S plus seven.' The Lipolian swapped every noun for another one seven words down in the dictionary."

Boucher knelt down. "Why here? Why this book?"

I shrugged off the question. In Coolidge, after all, authorship problems were common. Working with my dad, I'd encountered bookhackers, revisionists, demonstrative villains, bullying narrators, minor characters who wanted bigger roles, you name it. What did Boucher expect? These books were *worlds*, with families of characters that went back generations. They had a stake in the story and what happened next!

"How's your security?" I said.

Boucher's eyes were dead leaves. "*What* security?"

"I'd start there," I said. "Give Zell Hollister a call, tell her I sent you." Then I turned and started walking back across the page.

"Where are you going?" Boucher said.

"Back to work," I said. "I have a job, remember?"

"Wait a second," he stammered. "You've got to help me with this!"

"I said one hour," I said. "I've already put in way more than that. And I just told you what the problem was!"

"You haven't caught the Lipian yet, though."

"Lip-*o*-lian," I said, jumping the spine and walking toward the subway stop.

"_____!" shouted Boucher.

I didn't turn back. I left *Big Giant Floating Head* and made it back to Gar's by noon. Less than half an hour later I was on my way out to Blix to empty some traps. And they were full, too: I found four winged poems, all of them cold and dead.

· ✦ ·

In a corner of my mind I can still see my father falling: swinging his arms helplessly in the air, and then ceasing to swing them, just letting himself fall (Did he close his eyes? Did he think of me, or my sister, or my mother?) and landing on the page. He fell so far and so fast that his body made a divot in the fiber. They needed the story of a crane to remove him, plus stories about ambulances, paramedicones, Jaws of Life, the whole nine yards.

My mother arrived about thirty minutes later, and after sitting with me for an hour or so she tried to convince me to come home. But I wouldn't leave the scene—not even after they removed my father's body from the book and the ambulances and conecars sped away. I spent the night out there, on the dark page, with the bookwolves and wild poems, crying and shivering and praying to no one.

Three days later, we held a party—a French-Canadian wake—for my dad at the Denouement. If you've never been to a French-Canadian wake, it's a simple affair: everyone takes off their head and soaks it in a common vat of alcohol. Then you put your head back on, raise your fists and start swinging in honor of the dead. My mother fought her cousin. I fought my brother. My uncle fought a popcorn machine. You end up crying on the shoulder of the person you're trying to punch in the stomach.

· ✦ ·

I honestly never planned to return to *Big Giant Floating Head*. I went back to work at Gar's and I tried to forget all about sets and fiction and Bouchers. Which isn't to say I didn't miss it— miss being back in the book, wandering through the subtext, orchestrating behind the scenes, listening to the mysteries of the page. If I'm being honest, seeing my dad's last sets really affected me; he was more alive for me in those moments than he had been since the day he died. And the page *was* my true home. I mean that literally; my mother went into labor with me when she and my dad were living on location in a novel called *Winnebago*. I was born right there on page seven.

Later that fall, though, there was a fire in Boucher's book. Gar has a police scanner in the shop, and he heard the call go out; he radioed me in the van and I drove out to *Big Giant Floating Head* and right into the pages. I could see the fire—a golden glow over the spine, smoke rising past the page numbers—from as far off as page two. Luckily, the fire wasn't too bad; only five pages had burned before the fire department arrived to extinguish the blaze. But it could have been a disaster. When I got to the scene, the Narrative Inspector—Tony Lung, I knew him, good guy—was standing with his arms crossed while Boucher sat on the bumper of a fire truck breathing into an oxygen mask. Apparently Boucher had been trying to build sets *himself*. The pages behind him were a hissing mess, half of them browned from the fire, whole paragraphs ruined by water. Lung pointed over his shoulder. "My deputy says you had an electric reviser plugged into the spine of the book?"

Boucher took off the mask so he could speak. "I was just trying to— "

"Trying to what?" said Lung.

"—just fix one *sentence*," he said.

"Who's your electrician?"

"I was doing the work myself," said Boucher.

"Without a permit," said Lung.

I stepped up to Tony. "Ey, _____," he said.

"I just wanted to finish the story," said Boucher.

"You can't do any of this without *permits*."

"I didn't even know I needed one," Boucher said.

I suddenly understood. Back when my father was alive, he oversaw all of this stuff for Boucher: permits, narrative inspections, the approval of outlines, everything.

"What happened to Nehali?" I asked Boucher.

"Quit," Boucher said, and then held the oxygen to his face.

I put my hand on Lung's shoulder, walked him a few steps away from the page, and leaned in close to him. "What if I help here?" I said.

"I ought to shut him right down," Lung said. I could smell

cigarettes on his breath. "He could have destroyed the whole book!"

"Just, what if I see it through?" I said.

Tony put his hands on his waist and spat into the page. Then he nodded once and we walked back to the fire truck. "OK, Bowcher," he said. "_____ here's going to get you back on track."

Boucher jumped to his feet.

"He'll pull the permits and oversee the project. You don't write a fuckin' *word* without him. Understood?"

Boucher's face was bright. "Absolutely," he said.

"And if I have to come back here? I'm shutting you down for good."

·✦·

Boucher met me at Gar's the next morning and we got to work. First, I sent him to Readers' Tool and Supply. "Pick up a few good bookmarks," I said, "and some plotted tires. Some paper clips and a stapler. And where are your maps?"

He stared dumbly at me. "What maps?" he said.

"I'm going to need topographic and narrative, with character arcs included, and plot maps, too."

"I don't have any of that," he said.

I winced and shook my head. Then I hoisted my toolbox onto the workbench and started loading it up. I threw in some reading goggles, a thesaurus, and the folded-up Big Ear 9000.

"What's that?" Boucher said.

"The Big Ear 9000," I said. Then I unfolded the ear and strapped it to my head.

Boucher smirked.

"What?" I said.

"That's a really big ear," Boucher said.

Embarrassed, I unstrapped the ear. "You got a better way to scan the page?"

Boucher left for Readers' and came back with everything I'd asked for, and by that afternoon we had the van all packed up. When we'd finished loading the last box, I slammed the van's back doors closed and said, "I'll go in tomorrow, and I'll call you when I've got something. Until then, don't do anything dumb."

"Ten-four," Boucher said.

"I mean it," I said. "Write *smart*."

Boucher nodded. "I promise."

The following morning I woke up early, grabbed a coffee from Sorrow Roastery, and drove Gar's van back into the book.

· ✦ ·

Those first few days in *Big Giant Floating Head* were some of the toughest I'd had since my dad died. It was more difficult than I'd anticipated to be back in fiction, which I so closely associated with my father. Everywhere I looked I expected to see him: not only in the fragments of sets he built—the river in "DivorceLand," the office building in "Parade"—but in the sets he *might* have built, the scenes he could have constructed better or rendered more vividly.

Plus, it was soon clear that the Lipolian problem was bigger than I'd understood it to be. Everywhere I went—at least once every three or four pages—I found signs of it: equations written in the margin, random passages in French (*Le processus est le produit*," "*L'histoire est une fenêtre ouverte*"). Then, I was walking past the beginning of "Slippery" when I saw the letter "Y" discarded in a trash bin—which changed the title to "Slipper." Out of the kindness of my heart, I took out the letter and restored it. The next day, I was combing through an early draft of "Beautiful Outlaw" when I realized that some of the sentences were written in iambic tetrameter. I stood surprised among the words. I could not believe I'd been so duped! I found a phone booth in the story and dialed Boucher. "*Big Giant Floating Head,*" someone answered.

"Is Chris there?" I asked.

"Nope," he said. "He went out."

"Do you know where?"

"He's working in the Language Zoo this morning, I think," said the someone.

I dialed the Language Zoo. "Language Zoo."

"Chris Boucher, please," I said.

"Um, hold on a second. Can I ask who's calling?"

"It's _____," I said.

I heard the phone clunk down, and I waited a minute or two. Then Boucher picked up. "_____?" he answered.

"Yeah," I said. "Listen— "

"Did you catch him?"

"Not yet," I said. "Let me ask you something. Did you write any sentences in tetrameter?"

"What's tetrameter?" said Boucher.

So it must have been the Lipolian.

I chased that outlaw for over a month, driving my poetry truck from one chapter to the next with no sign of the culprit. Eventually I started to think I was tracking more than one Lipolian—that maybe I was tracking *all* of them, even!—or that it was just the words themselves, respawning and multiplying, that I was after.

Then, after five weeks in the book, I was hiking through the woods off the margin of "Trout Heart"—maybe three pages from the edge of what was written—when I saw, in the distance, a shadow in a paragraph. I tiptoed toward it, hid behind a tree, ran behind a page number, and then shuffled behind the post of an old rotted fence. When I got a page closer, I could see a person—a woman—standing in the language. She wore painter's overalls and there was ink all over her knees and shins. She had long, brown, braided hair, and she was kneeling in the words, smelling them like flowers. She was the most beautiful person I'd ever seen.

I didn't think the woman had heard me approaching, but suddenly she turned and stared at me and curtsied. "*Enchanté,*" she said.

I stopped in my tracks. She looked familiar. "What?" I said, dumbly.

"*Ça fait longtemps,*" she said.

She was speaking French—my father's language, which I didn't understand. But I knew its sounds—they were the sounds of home.

As I tried to figure out where I'd seen her before, she leaned over again and breathed deeply. Then she gestured to me, that I should do the same. So I did; I leaned down and inhaled. And the words smelled wonderful—rich and inky, with a mild, fruity aftertaste.

"*C'est bon, non?*" said the woman.

I didn't answer—I had my eyes closed, and I was taking deep gulps. It had been so long since I'd done that—decades, maybe. When had the page lost that sense of mystery for me? Finally, I opened my eyes; when I did I found that the Lipolian was gone, as if she'd never been there in the first place. I ran right over to where she'd been standing, but I could find no trace of her—no footprints in the ink, no wrinkles in the page.

I didn't tell Boucher about this—not then, and not afterward. After that first sighting, though, I doubled my efforts, immersed myself in the search. Instead of driving back out of the book every day, like I'd been doing those first weeks, I started sleeping right there in the story: first in hotels—I spent several nights at a place called The Tetherly—and if no hotel was nearby, in Gar's van or camped out in a tent wherever I could find a clearing on the page. Sometimes, if I was staked out, I slept right in that spot: I passed one whole night lying under a paragraph, and another crouched up behind a page number, shivering in the pagewind and waiting for the Lipolian to appear.

And she *did* appear, but never where I expected. When I was looking for her—in the middle of some weird syntax; at the story's climax—I never found her. But once, I was shopping for supplies at the Food Ellipsis and I saw her at the far end of the aisle. Another time, I was going down a mall escalator in "Success Story" and she was going up it. I jumped over the divider, of course, but by the time I got to the top of the stairs she was gone.

I should have realized earlier, though, that the Lipolian was fucking with me—sabotaging me, playing jokes at my expense. One morning, for example, she S + 7ed my breakfast—suddenly my oatmeal became Obadiah, a Hebrew minor prophet. She'd leave me notes, too. "Isn't it fun?" Or, "Just like the graveyard in *The Curtain!*" And now and again, I'd be scanning a page when, all of a sudden, the story became about *me*: *"I know _____ misses his father. We ALL miss Bellis."* Othertimes, she'd write the readers *into the work*, let them decide what happened to me:

If you want _____ to trip over a sentence and twist his ankle, keep reading this page.

If you want _____ to get lost in the subtext, stop reading here and turn to page 125.

If you want this story to be over, turn to page 128.

Suddenly I tripped over a sentence. "Ah!" I shouted. "My ankle!"

The farther out in the book I went, the more I struggled. Way out on page 120, for example, I was listening to the page with the Ear when I suddenly looked up and saw the *exact sentence* in reverse farther down the page, and and page the down farther reverse in *sentence exact* the saw and up looked suddenly I when glass magnifying my with page the reading and ear the wearing was I example for 021 page on out way. So that everything I wrote became a reflection of itself, like some sort of palindrome prose prose palindrome of sort some like itself of reflection a became wrote I everything that so.

Then, a few days later, I was scanning the page with the Ear 9000 when I came across a particularly thorny passage:

> It's just a curiously inky question from a motion-less, dead azalea mixing into the vapid, brown, soily ground.
>
> "Where and why?" says the bearded, kilted azalea that night, quietly gritting its teeth. "Why

can't I at least shuffle? Am I just—truly, verifiably dead? Me? Never exist again? As I speak, I've never been this sad!"

"But death is everywhere," said the callous tulip. "It's just that not one of us quite knows when they exist and when they don't—when they're standing in the hazy sun, or when they've been buried under ground."

"But I know that I'm living," said a pansy to our tulip. "I know if I'm in hazy sun, on Xanax, or just in clouds. And I'm not dying—not quitting, not now."

Halfway through these paragraphs, the Ear got very hot on my head and smoke started pouring out of the canal. I unstrapped it and let it cool on the page, but the Ear 9000 was finished—I'd burst the drum. Flummoxed, I walked back to my van. When I turned the key, though, nothing happened. I checked under the hood and saw that every part in the engine had been replaced with its word: "engine," "alternator," "battery," "spark plugs," et cetera. This, of course, was the work of the Lipolian.

"Goddammit!" I shouted to no one.

What could I do at that point, though, but press on? So I packed up some essential tools—my reading goggles, some edible words—boarded the subway, and rode it as far as it would take me. I'd been riding for about an hour, though, when suddenly—smack-dab in the middle of "DivorceLand"— the train stopped. I looked out onto the page and saw the end of the track. This was as far as Boucher had written; the pages ahead were discarded drafts, forlorn paragraphs, dead ideas. I pushed open the doors of the train, stepped onto the empty page, and started walking.

Did I understand, by that point, that the Lipolian was drawing me farther in? Of course I did. I knew it was a game, but I had to keep playing. So I trudged through the white space, past strange characters and occasional stories: a person who appeared to be all hair; a cancer; a crashed plane in the distance. Soon I lost track of my whereabouts—I couldn't tell how much time had passed. Later that day—or the next, who knows?—I heard an approaching engine in the distance and I turned to see Boucher's old black truck approaching. He drove across the page and pulled up right beside me. "Get in!" he shouted.

I ignored him. I was hungry, thirsty, half-blind from the pageglare.

"_____!" he shouted.

"No thank you," I said, marching on.

Boucher kept pace with me. "What happened to your van?"

"*Gar's* van," I said. "Broke down."

Boucher nodded. "_____," he said, "have you made any progress at all? Have you even *seen* the Lipian yet?"

"Lip-O-lian," I said. "And yes, I've seen her several times."

Boucher's truck coughed along in fits and spurts. "Listen," he said. "This has gone far enough. I think we should cut our losses and go home."

I huffed. "It's too late for that," I said.

"Look, _____," Boucher said. "I'm still the author here, and I am *ordering* you to call this off."

I stopped walking and leaned over the window so my face

was inches from Boucher's. "Leave me *alone*," I told him. "Turn your car around and drive away."

"Not unless you come with me," Boucher said.

I looked down to the ground and scanned the page—this paragraph—until I found the next sentence: It was "Boucher kept following me." I picked up the clause, snapped it in the middle, and started bending the letters.

"What are you doing?" Boucher said.

Then I put the sentence back on the page. Now it read, "Boucher turned around and drove home, and he never bothered _____ again." As soon as I placed it on the ground, the pickup turned around.

"Wait," Boucher said.

The truck sped back across the paper.

"No—stop. Wait, _____!" he said. But the truck carried him away, and soon I was alone again.

I trudged on for another full day, past the end of "Parade" and into the space beyond it. By that point I couldn't see a story at all—just random excerpts and tumbles of words here and there.

Was I in the subtext?

In a word desert?

Was I still the main character, even? Or had I wandered

into another story,
another book?

        as another character, maybe

                                      not

myself

    Sometime after that—I can't say how long—I heard another engine, this one in front of me. Then, in the distance, I saw a moving figure: someone riding a motorcycle.

    Before it reached me, though, I heard a loud *clang*. Then I bumped my face on something. It was a sentence: a vertical sentence.

Enough is Enough

    Then another appeared next to it—*clang* —and another.

You belong here. With us.

What would your father say?

I moved to my left: two more sentences. I turned to my right. *Clang. Clang. Clang.* Sentences lined up around me, behind me, above me. I was in a cage of sentences.

Then I saw the Lipolian, crossing over the page in the strang-
est vehicle I'd ever seen—it was a motorcycle made entirely of
verbs: an engine of go and handlebars of veer. She rode up to
the cage, dropped the kickstand, and climbed off her bike. I put
my hands on the bars—the sentences. "Let me out of here!" I
said.

She smiled. "Ce n'est pas ma cage," she said. "C'est le tienne."

"Do you know why I'm here?" I shouted. "To *exterminate*
you."

The Lipolian looked genuinely hurt. "You don't remember
me?" she said.

I shook my head.

"*Ou* my mother?" said the Lipolian. "Brigitte Remillard?"

Of course—she wrote C u b e. I suddenly remembered scaling
paragraphs with this girl, and painting letters different colors.
We were probably seven or eight.

"Your father?" she said, sitting down on the page. "Would
have wanted you *ici*." She pointed down to the page. "*Et là*—
there." She pointed to the blank page beyond her.

"My father's dead," I said.

"I know," she said. "But you were *born* on the page."

"I'm here now," I said.

"I mean for good," she said. "I mean, be *here*."

I looked ahead, at all the unwritten fiction. "I don't work in
stories anymore," I said.

"No?" She gestured to the words all around me.

"This is Boucher's story," I said. "I'm working for him."

She made a face. Then she said, "Leave Boucher behind. You can go wherever you want to."

"I see my father everywhere in here," I said, my voice trembling.

"I know," she said. "I see my mother, too." Then she stood up.

Don't go, I thought. "Wait," I said.

The Lipolian smiled softly. "I'll find you in the next book." She swung her leg over the vehicle. "Or the one after that." Then she started up the vehicle and drove way.

All at once, the vertical sentences fell to the page. I looked back at the pages I'd read thus far—at my life up to this point. I felt recharged. Reborn. Free. And I didn't want to go back— back to Gar's, back to Coolidge, back to my angry, lonely life. So I stepped over the broken bars and ran forward into the white space.

FOR SALE BY OWNER

Four months had gone by without an offer, so I was delighted to get a call from our realtor, Wanda, saying she had a potential buyer. "But there's a catch," she said.

"How much is the offer?" I said.

Wanda told me the amount.

"Not bad!" I said.

"But listen," Wanda said. "They want your experiences as part of the sale."

"I'm sorry?" I said.

"Your and your wife's experiences in the home."

"Of—they—wow," I said. "I've never heard of a buyer asking for that. Is that common?"

"No, but it happens," Wanda said. "Not all clients are comfortable with it, but some are."

As it happened, I was standing in the kitchen, right next to the place where my cousin Lucien bumped his head on a low ceiling.

"Which ones do they want?" I asked Wanda.

Wanda coughed. "The offer asks for all of them."

"*All* of them?"

"But again," Wanda said, "you should feel free to make a counteroffer, or decline altogether."

We had to bring Lucien to the hospital for stitches. He kept saying how embarrassed he was.

I asked Wanda, "Do you think it's a reasonable offer?"

"In this market? I think it's worth considering."

I breathed heavily into the phone.

"Talk with your wife and let me know," Wanda said.

I walked into the kitchen. "We've got an offer on the house," I said.

Liz held out her hands as if she'd just caught an invisible beach ball. "That's great!" she said. "How much!"

I told her. "But there's a catch," I said.

"A catch," she said.

"They want our *experiences* in the house, too," I said.

"OK," she said. "So?"

"That's six *years*."

"Frankly?" she said. "I think it's a blessing in disguise. All the shit we went through in this house? Who needs it?"

"We've had some wonderful times in this old house," I said.

"Which times, Chris?" my wife said. "The leaky ceiling? The truck on blocks in the yard?"

"What about—"

"The shouting match in the driveway? The mouse infestation?"

"How about after your surgery, when I made you breakfast? The sticky notes you'd leave for me every day? All of the *intimacy*?"

"Hey, they can have it," said my wife.

"I don't believe you," I said. "These are our *lives* we're giving away here."

"Out with the old, in with the new," Liz said.

That night after dinner I went down to the basement. It was filled to the brim with moments—so many that you could hardly walk around. There was my stint as a glass blower; the day I woke up and everything was slippery; my first-ever competitive failure. There was Liz, strumming her guitar, and her again, studying for the GRE at the kitchen table. There were the two of us talking late into the night on the deck. I sat down on the cold basement floor and studied one memory after another.

The following day I called Wanda with a counteroffer: a slightly higher price and all of our memories except twenty or so that I could not part with. Wanda called back later that day with the buyers' response: they didn't care about my fortieth birthday party or the Christmases, but they wouldn't buy the house without mine and Liz's intimacy and our arguments. "Seriously?" I asked Wanda. "Why would they event *want* those experiences?"

"A lot of buyers want a house that's really been *lived* in," she said.

Finally I conceded—we accepted the offer, bought a condo and hired a moving company. Then the movers broke two experiences—that time everything was slippery, and the last conversation I had with my father—moving them into a van. "Insurance will cover this," one of the movers assured me, as I knelt down in the driveway and sifted through shards of conversation.

But I don't remember if we ever did hear from the insurance company, or what happened to those broken memories, or anything else about the day we moved. I sold it all with the house, which I couldn't find now if my life depended on it. It's like I never even owned it. All I know for sure is that, before we lived here, we lived somewhere else.

TROUT HEART

That summer my heart told me that it was taking a vacation. "Not forever," it told me. "Just a few weeks of R and R."

I was driving through downtown Coolidge at the time, on my way to meet a Suicide in South Blix, and I forced a laugh—I thought the heart was kidding. "Right," I said.

"And I'll get a substitute while I'm gone, of course," said the heart.

"Wait a second—you're serious?" I said.

"Chris, I need a break," said the heart. "And it'll give us a chance to get perspective on our, shall we say, communication problems."

I was confused. "But you obviously can't *take a vacation*," I said. "I need you to breathe, and think, and live. Don't I?"

"Not necessarily. But I just told you, I'll get you a sub. I know just who to hire."

"A *substitute* heart?"

"Real freelance hearts charge a lot of money," said the heart. "But I know a trout who subs for hearts all the time."

My truck ambled down Route 11. "A literal trout? An actual fish?"

"Yes, a fish," said the heart. "An experienced trout heart substitute. You'll get along great—he's a good fish."

"If you *do* take a vacation—"

"*When* I take the vacation."

"—where would you go?" *What will you take from me this time?*

"I was thinking about going to the Cape," said the heart. "Renting a place in Truro. Eat some lobster, walk the beach."

"That sounds really nice," I said. "Why can't we both go?"

"Do you have the money for a trip like that?" said the heart.

"No," I said.

"Anyways, you're not invited. I'm going alone."

I took a left on Stress Ave. "I think it's a nice idea *in theory*?" I said. "But I need you here, working for me. So unfortunately I'm going to have to say no."

Now my heart forced a laugh. "Chris," he said. "Look back at the first sentence."

I looked into my rearview mirror, at the paragraphs behind me and the first sentence.

"Did you read it?" said the heart.

"Yes," I said.

"What's it say?"

"'That summer my heart,'" I said, "'told me that it was taking a vacation.'"

"Right," said the heart. "I'm not *asking* you; I'm informing you that I will be unavailable the week of June 21. *Capiche?*"

By that point we'd reached the concrete factory where I said I'd meet the Suicide. I parked and saw him sitting on some steps by a trailer. He had his tackle box and fishing pole at his feet, and he was reading a book. When he saw me, he stood up and stuffed the book into the front pocket of his overalls.

"Sorry I'm late," I said. "I was arguing with my heart."

The Suicide gave me a little shove. "Having a *heart-to-heart*?"

"Good one," said the heart to the Suicide.

We walked past giant concrete forms on the way to the river bank. This was the Coolidge River, a notorious story source. "Goddamn good spot, no?" said the Suicide.

I stood on the edge and peered into the water. Sure enough, I could see the stories swimming by in the murky brown among fish, stones, anonymous faces, and underwater vegetation. We baited our lines with conflict and cast them out into the water.

· ✦ ·

That was way back in 2004, about two years before I met Liz. I was engaged to a woman named Melody at the time, and writing every day. On the page, the whole world was smiling at me; I believed Coolidge—my Coolidge, and the Christopher Boucher(s) that moved through it—could be anything I wanted them to be. So when Melody sat me down to tell me that she'd been diagnosed with cancer and wanted to call off the wedding, I couldn't hear the words; I needed to revise them. "I'm so, so sorry," Melody said, leaning forward on our futon and holding my hands in hers. "For me, but also for you."

"No no no no no," said my thoughts. "*No.*"

"I want to know who this guy Cancer is, and where he lives," I said.

Melody smiled sadly.

"Honey," I said. "We can beat this."

"No," she said, staring at my knuckles as if she was reading them. "We can't."

"This is *our* Coolidge, Melody. *We* decide what happens—"

"And it's better if we just say goodbye now. I don't want you to worry about me, or what's next for me—I'd rather go through it alone." She looked up at me with tears in her eyes. "It would make me happy to know that you're out there in the world, being your good weird self." Then she kissed me—her breath tasted like paint—told me she loved me, stood up from the futon, and walked out of the apartment.

In the lonely hours afterward, my thoughts revised and revised until I decided that she was kidding. She'll walk in any second, I told myself, and rib me for being gullible. But she didn't come home that night or the next. After three days without her, I drove out to her parents' home in Geryk Heights. When I walked up to the front door it squared its shoulders. "Leave, Christopher," the door said.

"Hi," I said. "I'm here to see—"

"She doesn't want to see you," said the door. "Go. Now."

"Can you at least let her know I'm here?" I said.

"She's not to be disturbed under any circumstances," said the door.

"I'll just," I said, and I lifted my hand to knock, but the door said, "Don't. Don't you touch me, Christopher."

I knocked on the door's face.

"What did I just say?"

I slapped the door. "Melody!" I shouted.

"Do that again?" said the door. "And I'm calling the police."

I punched the door with my fist.

The door sighed and fished a cell phone from its pocket. As soon as he started dialing, I yanked my hands off the door as if it was a million degrees hot. Then I whirled around, stormed down the steps, got into my car, and drove away.

· ✦ ·

But that wasn't the end of The Story of Melody. In fact, it wasn't even the end of *this part* of the story, where I am trying desperately to see her. Other characters might have just given up at that point, moved on, turned the page, but my heart wouldn't let me. Melody promised me that she'd love me forever. And I knew I could save her if she gave me the chance. All I had to do, I told myself, was put the right words in the right order.

So the next day, I called in to the bookstore and said I was sick. "I'm not going to be able to come in—I'm really sorry," I told my boss, a Marsha.

"You don't sound sick," said a Marsha.

"I'm not congested," I said. "But I have other symptoms."

"Dammit, Christopher," a Marsha said, "we're running low on mysteries—I was counting on *you* to go catch some."

"Send the Verb!"

"Verb is the worst!" she said. "Last time he came back with an empty bucket!"

"Send Om."

"Om is on the register," she said.

"How about Never?" I said.

"Screw it, I'll go out myself," she said.

Half an hour later I drove my truck back to Melody's house and parked it on the street a few blocks away. Thankfully the door was asleep, gently snoring on the front steps, so it didn't see me or hear me. I sat in the car and read a novel that I'd taken out of the bargain bin at the store—one that was so weird, no one would buy it. A week earlier, I'd held it up to a Marsha on the way out the door to go catch stories—I was looking for something to read by the riverbank. "Can I borrow this?" I said.

"Take it, keep it," she said.

"You sure?" I said.

"Please—you'd be doing me a favor," she said.

· ✦ ·

Later that afternoon, the garage door finally yawned and Melody's Hyundai drove out. I put down my book, started my car, and followed her—down the street, onto 201, to a parking lot about a mile away. She parked and walked into a big building made of red stone. There was a sign out front that read "St. Paul's."

What was she doing at a church? And what would happen if I followed her inside? It had been so long since I'd been inside a church that I didn't really remember how they worked. Was there an admission fee? I didn't have any money. I mean it—not a single dime. My car ran on the memory of gasoline.

"Should I go in?" I asked my heart.

"Into the church? Absolutely *not*," my heart said. "You shouldn't even *be* here, Chris."

"I'm going to go see what's happening in there," I said.

"She's probably a member of this church," said my heart. "And you're not—you don't belong."

"Where *do* I belong?" I asked him.

"That's not what I mean," said my heart.

I got out of the car and walked up to the big wooden doors. "Blessed be," one said to me.

"OK," I said.

"Are you here for the meeting?" asked the other door.

"Yes," I said, and both doors swung open.

．✦．

On the other side was one of the most beautiful rooms I'd ever seen, with rows of big wooden benches and colorful windows and a big elaborate stage in the front. The room could have held hundreds of people, but right now there were only fifteen or twenty, all of them sitting in the front two or three rows of benches. Several of the people—the women, even—were bald; one person was in a wheelchair. They were all focused on a heavy-set woman who was standing on the floor in the center aisle, saying something that I couldn't hear.

I looked for Melody, and spotted her on the far right side. As I was watching her watch the speaker, the big doors opened again and three more people walked in and passed by me. I followed them down the left aisle and into the fourth row of benches. I ended up sitting next to a woman with a yellow bandanna on her head.

I couldn't really follow what the speaker was saying: something about people being connected, with occasional mentions of God. Then she said, "I want to try something. OK? Just bear with me here. I want you to take hold of the hand of the person next to you."

The woman with the yellow bandanna took my hand. On the other side of the room, Melody turned to her left to speak to her neighbor; when she did, she saw me across the aisle. Her face ghosted and she stood up and stormed out of the church.

I would have gone after her, but I didn't want to offend the woman holding my hand. She was looking at the stage and whispering, "I don't know. I don't know."

"Don't know what?" I whispered.

"I don't know," she said, over and over again. And she was squeezing my hand really tight, as if she was trying to suck the livingness from my body to hers.

"Pssst," I said to my heart.

"What?" it said.

"Go find out where Melody's going."

"Fuck you," said my heart. "I will not contribute to the trouble you're causing that woman. Isn't she suffering enough? Can't you just let her go?"

The woman squeezed my hand, and I squeezed back. I lived inside that squeeze for a moment. *This* is where I belong, I thought. This is my home, right here in this story. But then the speaker told us we could let go of each other's hands, and we did, and I was alone again, and there was no home, and there never had been and never would be.

The speaker continued on about salvation, and heaven, and many other ideas that I had trouble following. Soon I lost track of what she was saying. I felt tired and bored. Plus, I had to go to the bathroom.

I turned around to look for doors marked with the bathroom sign—the blocky man with the round head, the triangle skirt of the woman—when I noticed a balcony at the back of the room. What was up there? It was dark on the balcony, but as I looked closer, I thought I saw—

Was that a face?

I looked closer.

Then I saw it blink. It *was* a face.

There was someone up there, staring down at us—at me.

The speaker finished and everyone clapped and stood up. People began to talk in groups, and a woman with a clipboard approached me. "Is this your first time here?"

"In a church?" I said.

She smiled. "At the support group," she said.

As I spoke with her, I saw the man from the balcony—that face, and a very thin body dressed in overalls and a flannel shirt—moving up the side aisle toward the front. I read his eyes as he passed me.

"Do you want to leave your contact information?" the clipboard lady asked me.

"What for?" I said.

"So we can send you news and updates," she said.

I wrote down my email address, bowcherbooshay@gmail .com. "S-H-A-Y?" said the woman. I said yes. "I don't have a computer," I said. "I can only get my email at work." She handed me some brochures and she moved on to someone else.

I walked up to the stage and found the thin man behind a big table, on his hands and knees. "Excuse me," I said.

"What are you doing?" my heart shouted into my mind. "Do you know what that is?"

The thin man looked up.

"Are you—praying?" I said.

He shook his head. "Cleaning," he said.

"Stop talking to that thing right now!" my heart said. "Don't you know it's a Suicide?"

Of course I did—I knew a Suicide when I saw one. I watched him scrubbing some substance on the floor. "Is that blood?" I said.

"Somebody puked back here," he said.

"Nice of you to clean it," I said.

"Nice has nothing to do with it," he said. "It's my job."

"You're a janitor?"

"Building maintenance," he said, standing up.

"What a cool building to maintenance," I said.

He laughed. "Think so?" He took out a flask and brought it to his lips. He must have seen me eye it, because he looked down at the flask and then held it out to me. "Sip?" he said.

"What is it?" I said.

"Watered-down death," he said.

"No," said my heart to my mind. "No, Chris."

But another part of me figured, why not?

"Because it's *death* is why not," said my heart.

I took a sip. The room went shaggy and low.

"What's your name, pardner?" said the Suicide.

"Christopher," I told him.

· ✦ ·

The next day I went back to work at AquaBooks. Usually they sent me out story catching, but some days, like today, I worked in the shelves. Once, years earlier, I'd owned a bookstore. But I couldn't manage it—I lost it all investing in expensive, experimental texts. Luckily, a Marsha knew my uncle, and called me after I closed the store and offered me a job. We sold all kinds of books at AquaBooks—lakebooks, streambooks, pondbooks, oceanbooks, puddlebooks, you name it.

That morning, my mind was still turning from the drink I'd shared with the Suicide, and I knew that a Marsha could see something floating in my eyes. Also, I felt nauseated—I could still feel that death sloshing around in my belly. I decided, right then and there, that I would not go back to the church. Religion just didn't sit right with me, apparently.

But later that week, the Suicide walked right into Aqua-Books; I was ambling out of the stockroom, with my story-catching equipment in hand, and he stepped out of the stacks. "Hey," he said.

"Oh," I said. "Hi again."

"Remind me of your name?"

"Christopher," I said.

"I didn't know you worked here," he said. Even though, when I drive back to those old paragraphs? I *distinctly remember* telling him that I worked at AquaBooks. "What are you doing here?" I asked.

"Browsing," he said. "I think I found a good one." He held up a book called *The God of the Martians*. "Do you know it?"

I shook my head. "But it looks interesting."

The Suicide put the book under his arm. "You should come back to St. Paul's," he said.

"To the support group?"

The Suicide shrugged. "Or just—to hang out, shoot the shit. I'm there every night," he said.

I said I'd try, and I shook his hand and left to go catch stories. As soon as I stepped out of the store, though, my heart started nagging me. "Suicides are not good people, Chris," said my heart. "Not people at all, actually. They want different things than you or I want. Right?"

"Right," I said.

"You don't sound very convinced."

"   "

"Chris?"

"What?" I said.

"Things aren't that bad. Are they?"

"They aren't good," I said.

"You're just upset about Melody," said the heart. "But hanging out with a *Suicide* is not going to help any. I want you to promise me we won't go back to St. Paul's."

"I won't."

"Promise."

"Cross you and hope to die," I said.

The heart nodded in my chest. "Now let's go catch a story," he said.

· ✦ ·

Catching a story is simple: you just go out to a river and cast your line. The best stories lie at the bottom of streams, lakes, or oceans. To find a good spot for stories, look for the faces—the old lives now fictioned. Hook a character or sentence and reel it in. Then you dry it out, bind it, and put it on the shelves.

Of course, you have to read the water. Every river and stream works differently. Some rivers—rivers without story—are actually swimmable! Other streams, though, are very magazine. And those that contain stories, or memories? You can't expose yourself to that water unless you yourself are ready to be memoried and storied.

I spent that whole day on the Coolidge River, catching until dusk. Late in the afternoon, I put my bucket of stories in my truck and drove back to Aqua. By the time I dropped the stories off it was almost eight o'clock. When I got back in the car, I felt a pang of loneliness. I tried to ignore it, and started driving home, but the car—it was the *car*, I swear it was—steered us towards Geryk. By the time my heart figured out what was happening we were already on 117. "Wait a second," he said. "Chris. Where are you going?"

"It's not me," I said. "It's the car. It's driving of its own accord!"

"Bull*shit*," said my heart. "You promised, Chris."

"It's out of my control!" I lied.

My heart slunk down and went silent; I could feel it crossing its arms in my chest.

When I walked into the church, I found the Suicide playing the organ. "Ey!" he said. "It's the storycatcher!" He stood up and handed me a chalice with some death in it. I took a sip. "Want the tour?" he said.

"Sure," I said.

He walked me behind the stage, through a series of rooms and offices. One closet was full of chirping robes. Another room held books in different languages. "This is the pastor's office," said the Suicide. He collapsed into a leather chair and I sat down across from him. "Haven't seen you at the support group," he said.

"No," I said.

"I saw your friend, though. Melanie?"

"Melody," I said.

"What's going on with her health?" he asked.

"Chris," said my heart, through clenched teeth. "Don't you tell him anything about Melody."

"That group?" said the Suicide. "Is for people with terminal cancer."

"Melody's fine," I said, revising. "She isn't even sick. She's going to live forever."

· ✦ ·

That was the first of many nights that summer that I hung out with the Suicide—I'd stop by with fast food or a six-pack, and we'd mix the beer with death and sit in the pews and get fucked up. Once, the Suicide dared me to eat all of the communion wafers and I did it. Another time, he climbed the cross on the back wall to see how high he could get. He made it almost to the top before the wall mounts started to whine, and then the Suicide leapt off and landed on the floor.

Maybe two weeks into my church visits, we were sitting in the benches with our feet up, not really talking, when the Suicide dug into his pocket and said, "Hey. Want to try something?"

"What?" I said.

"Here."

There were two gold bullets in his palm.

"What are those?" I said.

"Bullets, dummy," he said. He tossed one up in the air and caught it in his mouth. "Now you," he said, and he held out a bullet.

"Really?" he said.

"You suck it until it explodes."

"Absolutely not, Chris," said my heart.

I put the bullet in my mouth.

"Do you listen to anything I say, ever?" said the heart.

The bullet tasted foul.

"Wait for it," said the Suicide. His face was a holiday.

I let the bullet sit in my cheek. It grew warm, and hot, and hotter.

"Spit it out," said my heart.

Then I heard a noise from the Suicide—a crack inside his mouth—and his eyes went wide. "And the world is: beautiful," he said. He spit the casings out on the bench.

"Christopher Gerard Victor Boucher, you spit that bullet out right now or *we are dead*," said my heart.

The bullet was hot on my tongue. I could feel holes forming in my mind.

"Chris!" shouted my heart.

I spit out the bullet.

"Aw," said the Suicide. "Boo. Hiss."

"I'm fine without the explosion," I said.

"But the explosion is the *juice*!" he said.

"No thanks," I said.

"You need to be willing to *lose*," said the Suicide.

I said, "Lose what?"

"Everything," he dreamed.

"I lost the only woman who ever loved me—I couldn't lose more if I tried," I said.

The Suicide lay down on the bench. "*Loved* you. What does that word even *mean*?"

"What? It means—" I said, but I don't think I said anything else. I was having trouble focusing—trouble seeing, even. I slumped over onto my side.

I passed out right there in the pew. I woke up the next

morning to the sound of the organist opening the double doors. The Suicide was gone—there were just a bunch of shell casings where he'd been. I put them in my pocket and ran out the fire door.

· ✦ ·

Maybe a month after I met the Suicide, Melody died. At least, that's what the email from the support group said. When I showed up to the funeral home, the room for Melody's party was crowded with people. The front door saw me and walked right over. I could tell he'd been crying. "Christopher," he said. "*Shorts*, Christopher?"

I looked down at my pale legs, then back up at the door. "Where is she?"

The front door took a deep breath, put his arm around me, and walked me up to a big closed box in the center of the room. We both stared at the golden box.

"Where's Melody?" I asked.

The door nodded toward the box. Then he nudged me toward Melody's family, who were standing a few feet away, all in a row. Her father hugged me and said, "She loved you, Christopher. She really did love you. She just didn't want you, or any of us, to suffer."

"That's what I want to ask her about," I told him. "Do you know where I can find her?"

"Chris!" scolded my heart.

"What?" said her father.

"Just tell me where she is," I said.

"You're an asshole, Chris," said my heart.

The front door led me swiftly to the back of the room. I was shouting now: "Where's Melody! Can anybody tell me? I want to see my fiancée! *Right! Now!*"

Everyone was staring. The door motioned to the garage door and a shed, and the three of them carried me out of the funeral home.

· ✦ ·

My heart didn't talk to me for three days after that. When he finally did, on our way to meet the Suicide for a storycatch, it was only to tell me he was leaving town. "So even my *heart* is against me now," I told the Suicide as we cast out our lines.

"Selfish *heart*," said the Suicide, reeling in the conflict. "In your time of need, no less." He took a sip from his flask and handed it to me, but I waved it away. "Got any bullets?" I said.

He gave me one and I popped it into my mouth. He ate one too. After a minute I said, "Is it flavored?"

The Suicide nodded. "Watermelon," he said. I heard his bullet explode in his mouth. And then the Suicide did something very strange: he walked to the very edge of the bank, so that the memories were only a foot away from his shoes. "What are you doing?" I said.

Without another word, he put down his storycatcher and jumped into the water.

"No!" I shouted. This river was *teeming* with stories, and even a few whole novels—it was very harmful to swim in. I spit the bullet out and ran to the edge of the bank. For a moment I thought the Suicide was dead—I couldn't see him, and I was sure that he'd been memoried. Then he surfaced, his hair slicked back and his eyes alight.

— 148 —

"What are you *doing*?" I shouted.

"What?" he hollered. "It's so refreshing!"

"Doesn't it hurt?"

"What?"

"The water?"

"Why would it?" he shouted.

"Because of the stories?" I shouted.

The trout's name was Tod. With one D. My heart made arrangements for him to arrive on a Monday morning that August. Sure enough, I heard the spit of an engine outside my apartment that morning and I looked out the window and saw a trout riding a motorcycle into the driveway of the apartment house. I went outside and opened my shirt and my heart jumped out. He and the fish did this weird handshake, and then my heart turned to me and said, "And this—this is Chris."

The fish nodded. "Ah. The funeral crasher, yes?"

"I'm sorry?" I said.

The heart flashed the trout a look, and the trout gestured to my chest. "May I?" he said.

I planted my feet and the fish jumped into my empty heart cavity. I could feel him shifting and settling. Then he said, "How's that feel?"

"Weird," I said.

"It'll probably take some getting used to," said the heart.

"We'll be fine," the fish told the heart.

The heart checked his watch. "Well," he said. "I'm going to hit the road. Miles to go before I sleep and all that." The heart got on the fish's motorcycle and started it up.

"He's taking your motorcycle?" I asked the fish.

"Yup," said the heart.

"He's *borrowing* it," said the fish.

"Right," said the heart. "I'm just borrowing it."

"And bringing it back in the exact same condition. Or else he's going to get his ass kicked by a school of pissed-off trout hearts."

"Are you absolutely sure about this?" I asked the heart.

The heart revved the engine and kicked the clutch. "Chris?" he said. "I've never been more sure of anything in my life."

"I'll see you next week," I said. In my mind, some of my thoughts started to cry. The heart waved to me. "I love you," I told him, but he was already driving away.

·✦·

The trout heart was different than my biological heart, but I liked him. First, he was a big reader. My biological heart hadn't read a full book in years, but the trout spent all of his free time reading. That night, in fact, I lay on my back on my broken futon and we—the trout and I—read the same book simultaneously. It was a new waternovel called *The Complete Absence of Twilight*. We both read the entire novel, and then we discussed it. I found it pretty abstract, but the trout said he liked that aspect of it.

When I woke up the next morning, though, the fish was gone from my chest. I spent ten minutes looking for him—I checked the bathroom, the kitchen, the basement—before I looked out the window and saw the trout heart jogging up the street toward my apartment.

I ran outside. "What the hell?" I shouted.

"What?" he said.

"I woke up and you weren't here," I said.

"So?" he said. "My hours are eight a.m. to midnight. From 12:01 to 7:59, I'm my own fish."

"And what about me?"

"What about you?"

"What do I do when you're not here?"

"Make do! What did you think, that I'd work for you twenty-four hours a day? Have no life of my own?"

While my biological heart spent most of its time in my chest, the trout heart was probably in my chest only fifty percent of the time. If we were out storycatching, for example, he'd often jump down and walk around a little. A few times, he even cast a line to catch a few stories.

"What are you doing?" asked the Suicide, who was standing downstream.

The trout said, "What do you *think* I'm doing?"

"A fish catching stories?" said the Suicide.

"Got a problem with that?" said the trout.

"Just never seen it, is all."

"I can't imagine there's much *you* haven't seen," the trout said.

·✦·

With the trout heart in my life, though, I went to St. Paul's less than before. The following week, in fact, I didn't go at all. That Wednesday, the Suicide called my cell phone. "Christopher?" he said. "You coming by?"

"Not tonight," I said. "We're just sitting at home and reading."

"We?" said the Suicide.

"Me and the trout," I said.

"Hi," said the trout heart into the phone.

"I've got fresh bul-lets!" sang the Suicide.

"No thanks," I said.

"You sure?" said the Suicide.

"Maybe another time," I told him.

· ✦ ·

Two or three days later, the Suicide came to AquaBooks during my shift. He walked right up to me where I was shelving books in the Romance section and grabbed my elbow. "Christopher," he said.

I twisted around; the Suicide's overalls were dirty and his face was a sale.

"Hey," I said. "Sorry I haven't called you back."

"I found her, Christopher."

"Who?" I said.

"Melody."

"Melody?"

"Yeah. I found her. I was out catching stories and I found her."

"Where?" I said.

"I can't tell you," he said. "But I can show you."

"Why can't you tell me?"

"It's out past the Gorges," the Suicide whispered. "But it'd be impossible for you to find her without me."

"Does she still want to marry me?"

A light flashed in his eyes. "You can ask her that yourself when you see her."

Then a Marsha called me to the front desk, and I told the Suicide that I had to go.

"Call me," he said. "Today. OK?"

• ✦ •

And I was just about to call him, on the walk back to my apartment that night, when the trout heart stopped me. "I really don't think that's a good idea," he said.

"Did you hear what he said about Melody?"

"And you trust him?" said the trout.

"Of course I do. He's a friend of mine," I said.

The fish snorted. "Suicides aren't *anyone's* friends," he said. "He's just pretending to be your friend so that you'll—you know."

"So that I'll what?"

"You know what a suicide *is*, right?"

"Yes," I said.

"Is that what you want? To kill yourself?"

I shrugged. "No. I don't know."

"Stop for a second," he said. "Sit down."

By that time we were right near the corner of Main and Pearl. I found a metal bench and sat down.

The fish said, "Do you mind if I try something?"

"That depends on what it is."

"I'm going to take a look at your missing."

"In my mind?"

The trout nodded.

"Right here?"

"If that's OK," the trout said.

"Will it hurt?"

"Not at all."

"As long as it doesn't hurt," I said.

The trout began moving through my body, right there as I sat on that bench. He swam up through my chest cavity, past my lungs, through my neck, and into my skull. Soon I could feel him swimming around inside my mind. "Wow," he said.

"Wow what?" I said.

"Nothing," he said.

"What do you see?"

"It's just, there are some serious gaps between one thought and the next."

Then he didn't say anything for a while. I looked up and down Main Street, and tried to think something intelligent so that the trout would see the thought. The City of Coolidge, I thought, is a pair of sandals.

"How is Coolidge a pair of *sandals*?" said the fish. Then I felt him swim across to the other lobe, and he said, "Wait a second. Hold on. I think I found something here."

"What?" I said.

"Oh jeez, Chris."

"What? What do you see?"

He swam back through my neck and into my chest and leapt out onto the bench. "Chris. Melody didn't *choose* to have cancer—you know that, right?"

"This is *my* story—*my* Coolidge," I said, my voice quivering. "And *I* make the rules. No one dies here unless I say they do."

The fish rolled its eyes. "I'm sure she loved you, Chris. But it sounds like she was really sick. That's probably why she—"

"She *still* loves me," I said. "And we're going to be reunited." I fished in my pocket until I found my cell phone.

"Melody is dead, Chris," said the fish. "You attended her funeral, for Chrissakes!"

I dialed the Suicide. "Did you see that memory in my mind?" I asked the fishheart.

Tod nodded.

"And did you actually *see* Melody at the funeral?"

"But that's because—"

"Hello?" said the Suicide.

"I want to see her," I said.

"I knew you would," said the Suicide. Then he gave us directions to the place where he'd found her. "It's not far from my cabin, actually," the Suicide said.

I'm not sure exactly what town he led us to—someplace past Blix, to a road that was covered with trees that moved aside as we reached them. We turned onto it and the trees folded over the road behind us. Soon the road dead-ended, and that's where we found the Suicide, standing in a clearing and chatting with a tree.

The fish jumped out of my chest and onto the grass. "Quite a spot," he said.

"Pretty stunning, right?" said the Suicide. Something about him was different today—his face was shiny, his voice a blade.

"How do you know about this place?" I said.

"I told you, because I live out here," he said.

"Really," said the trout heart. "I assumed you lived near the church."

The Suicide shook his head. "I'm about a mile that way." Then he looked to me. "Ready?"

"I am," I said.

"I think I'm going to stay here," said the trout.

I shot him a look. "You sure?"

"Suit yourself," said the Suicide.

"Why don't you come along?" I said.

"Nah," said the fish. "I'll guard the truck—it's got all of our stuff inside."

The empty cavern of my chest echoed.

"Let's boogaloo," said the Suicide.

I tried to catch the trout heart's eye as we started down the crinkly path, but the fish was already moseying over to a nearby creek. I turned back to the Suicide, who was moving quickly down the zigzag trail. Soon we were far from the truck, and deep in the if of the forest, where the insects spoke a different language and the trees clung nervously to the steep sides of the bank.

"How long have you lived here?" I said, just to make conversation.

"All my life," said the Suicide. Then he said, "How are things going with that trout heart?"

"Fine," I said.

"He's kind of conceited, don't you think?"

I didn't respond.

We walked for another few minutes, and then I had to stop and rest. "Melody's out *here*?" I said, hunched over to catch my breath. "Really?"

"Just up the way," said the Suicide, and he continued on down the trail.

A few hundred yards farther, he stopped and turned back to me. "We're here," he said. Then he stepped onto a giant red rock that jutted out over a turbulent waterfall. "Look down," he said.

I looked down. I could tell, right off the bat, that the water was tainted. "What's the story with that water?"

"What's it look like?" he said.

"It looks like death," I said.

"Exactamundo," he said.

"Is this where you get it?"

The Suicide nodded. "This river flows right by my cabin. I just scoop it right into my flask."

"Wow," I said.

"Isn't it beautiful?"

I nodded. The death *was* sort of beautiful.

The Suicide slapped my shoulder. "Do you want to see Melody?"

I said yes, I did.

He led me to the other side of the giant rock. "See down there?" he said.

I didn't.

"Look closer, Christopher," he said.

I looked.

"Lean over. See?"

I leaned over.

"See?"

"Yes," I said.

I saw memories in the water below: faces and moments and

the storied idea of those moments. And among the dead, off to the right, was a face that did look like Melody's. Have I told you how stunning Melody was? Her face was a Sunday in the spring. Her skin was greenish under the water, though, and her light brown hair moved with the current.

Then I felt a push, and I fell and landed in the water—in the death. The first thought I had was, I'm fictioning—I'm dying. A cold, stabbing pain—an inner scream—began in my extremities and traveled through me.

I swam to the surface. The Suicide was treading death alongside me. "I told you you'd see her again," he said. "Right? Didn't I tell you?"

It was all clear. I was dying—I would be dead soon. "Please," I said to the Suicide. I reached for the shore.

"Just let yourself sink down," said the Suicide.

I looked below me. Melody's face was so close.

But then a line dropped from above. I looked up and saw the fish, the trout heart, with my storycatcher—one that I'd stowed in the back of my truck. Now *I* was the story he was catching. "Grab the line," said the trout heart.

I grabbed it and the fish pulled me up—the fish fished me out. He hauled me onto the riverbank, but I could hardly move—there was something wrong with my arms and my legs.

The Suicide appeared next to us. "What are you doing?"

"Saving this man," said the trout.

"*I* was saving him," said the Suicide. "Just like I saved her."

The trout heart put me over his shoulder and hustled me down the path.

"He wanted to be with her!" shouted the Suicide.

"*You* wanted him to be with her," the trout yelled back. "This story never had anything to do with him."

My left arm was—and is, and will always be—completely fiction. There was death in my ears, in my eyes, in my mind. "Am I going to die?" I said.

The trout said, "Do you want to die?"

"No," I said.

"Then you won't," said the fish, and he started running faster.

Am I still the main character, even?

· ✦ ·

I'd like to end this story by reporting that the Suicide was killed—that the trout took out his heart or something. But that would be a different, better story. This story is, we got into my truck and we drove out of the gorge. But halfway home, on a ridiculous hill on 143, we broke down and had to call a friend of the trout's to pick us up.

My legs healed, and the death drained from my eyes and ears and mind. The only fiction remaining is my left arm—everything from the shoulder down is invented.

Even so, I understand what happened now. She wanted to marry me—she did. But she died. She loved me, and then she died.

My heart was supposed to return at the end of that week, but it didn't. The trout heart stayed with me for an extra day, and then had to move on to another client. He called my heart's cell phone and left an irate message about his motorcycle. Then the trout heart took a cab to the train station.

In the months that followed, I tried filling my chest cavity with other things—fresh flowers, two birds, a stone. I wanted something that reminded me I was still alive. The following spring, I went to the Squeeze Box in Patience and bought a small, used melodica. It was blue and plastic and it wheezed notes every time I took a breath.

But then, one day about a year later, I was sitting at my kitchen table, trying to work on my novel, when I heard a sound in the distance. I stood up just in time to see a heart-driven motorcycle gurgling up the drive.

DIVORCELAND

That summer, my wife sat me down at the kitchen table, started to cry, and told me she couldn't be married to me any longer. "I'm sorry," she said. "I'm so sorry, Chris."

I took her hands in mine. "Can't we fix this?" I said. "We can fix this!"

My wife shook her head. "It's too late."

"No it isn't," I said. "We could go on a vacation. Or see a therapist!"

"But it's already happening, Chris," she said.

"What is?"

"The divorce," she said, and she nodded out the window. When I looked outside I saw the arms of our house hammering a for-sale sign into the lawn. As soon as the sign was in the ground a car pulled up to the curb. A man and a woman got out; they looked like us but younger. They said something to the house and the house extended its hand. The man and woman both shook it. Then a moving truck pulled up.

I ran outside. "What's going on out here?" I said to the house.

"We've been drifting apart for a while," said the couple in unison, and they walked past me and into the house.

"That's because you said you needed space," I called out to them.

"I did need space," said one of the movers, carrying a sofa toward me.

"And I still do," said the sofa. "That's what this whole thing's about."

"But we were happy," I said to the sofa. "Weren't we happy?"

"I haven't been happy for years, Chris," said my street.

I ran out to the curb. "Years?" I said.

A bus pulled up. "Two years at least," said the bus. I stepped onto it.

"Remember the Brandels' party?" said a woman sitting toward the front.

"No," I said.

"How you asked me what was wrong and I began to cry?" said an old man in the back.

I walked back to where he was sitting. "I know things haven't been perfect," I told him.

"Not *perfect*?" said a field out the window. "I'm a *shell* of myself, Chris."

I pressed the yellow strip behind the seat and the bus stopped; I got off and walked out into the field. "Every marriage has ebbs and flows," I said to the field.

"Please—you're making this more difficult than it needs to be," said a river through the trees.

I ran out to the river. "Honey, I'll change," I told the water.

"I'm not asking you to change," said the sun. "I'm asking you to let me go." Then it fell behind the water.

"But you're my whole life," I said to the sunset.

"You'll start a new life," said some new stars.

"Look me in the face and tell me you don't love me any-more," I said.

"I don't," said the moon, and it leaned down so that its face was an inch from mine. "I'm so sorry. But I don't love you any-more." Then the moon kissed me on the cheek, turned away from me, and left me alone in the dark.

THE BOOK *BIG GIANT FLOATING HEAD*

One afternoon, not long after my divorce, I came back to my room at the Baystate rooming house and found my door flung open. I'd been robbed! When I searched my room to see what was missing, though, I found my banjo where I'd left it and next month's rent still hidden in the bureau.

Then I looked in my desk drawers. I found my extra pair of glasses, my passport, my—wait, where was my manuscript?

My novel was gone!

I ran downstairs and knocked on the Knee's door. He answered. "Ey!" he said. A big cigar stuck out from between his teeth.

"Did you go into my room?" I said.

"No," he said.

"Someone came in and took the novel," I said.

"The one you read me? Big floating whatever?"

"*Big Giant Floating Head*," I said. "It's *gone*."

"Maybe the writing escaped," he said. "Did you consider that?"

"No way," I said. "Someone came in and stole it." It was true that my writing would sometimes cry, or stamp its feet in anger, or kick against the wood when I locked it in the drawer. The chapter "Success Story" had once staged a hunger strike, and another time "Beautiful Outlaw" purposefully knocked over my cup of chai from Coffee or Else. But *escape*? The writing wasn't smart enough. "That novel is worth everything to me," I said.

The Knee puffed on his cigar. "I'll ask Crab. If someone jacked it, Crabby will know about it."

But I never heard back from the Knee or Crab, nor did I see those pages again. Eventually, I chalked their loss up to my terrible Boucher luck—the same luck that sank my bookstore, put this wall in my mind, got me fired from the Department of Fiction, and almost killed me as a prayor.

But then, a few years later, I was working at Coolidge Heating and Air when we were called to Punch-Out Books in nearby Success to repair their ventilation system. We got reports that anger was flooding into their store. Early that Saturday, my boss Linda, her stepson What, and I drove over to the bookstore to see what the problem was. We climbed up onto the roof, found the AC, and took off the service panel. Linda spotted the problem immediately. "Ah, see?" she said. "Moodilator."

"What?" said What.

"Right here," she said.

We went down into the bookstore. Punch-Out Books sold all kinds of books, but they were best known for their extensive catalog of physical books: novels that patted you on the shoulder, essays that hugged you, poems that high-fived you, and a few rare editions of story collections that would literally punch you right in the face.

It had been years since I'd worked in books, but my thoughts still swooned a little in bookstores. Soon my thoughts were telling stories to each other about working in the Department of

Fiction, and storycatching at AquaBooks, and building stories from the ground up. "Remember Boris Sarah?" said one. "And Bellis?" said another.

In the stacks, meanwhile, all the customers were furious. They rifled through the books angrily and complained to each other about the prices. "Where is *Rolltop Desk*?" I heard one customer ask an employee.

"I don't fucking know what that is," said the bookseller.

"It's a poetry collection by Dalton Day," said the customer.

"Good for Dalton Day," said the bookseller.

Linda, What, and I approached the front desk and asked for Royale, the owner. Soon she came floating across the floor. I knew Royale well—she was infamous in the Coolidge book scene. Still, after all these years, she was stunningly beautiful: her dark skin was covered with tattoos of words, and her hair had books braided right into it. Once, I'd asked Royale out for dinner, and she said, "Seriously?"

"Yeah," I said. "Would you like to have dinner with me?"

"Bowcher," she said, "that's the funniest thing I've heard in months."

"Hey Bowcher," she said to me now. "What are *you* doing here?"

I shrugged. "Working for Coolidge Heating now."

"Good for you." She smirked and looked down at her shoes, as if trying not to openly laugh. Then she looked back up at Linda. "So what's the story?"

"Bad moodilator," said Linda.

Royale winced. "Again?" she said. "That one's less than two years old!"

"What?" said What.

— 166 —

Just then, a man no thicker than a sheet of paper approached the counter with a bunch of books. I glanced over at them and read their titles: *Where is the Closest Outlet?*, *The Palindrome Murders*, *Big Giant Floating Head*, *Prairie Justice*—

"Wait a second," said a thought in my mind.

"*Big Giant Floating Head?*" said another thought.

"It's completely fried," Linda was saying. "That's why you're venting so much anger."

As Royale started ringing up the books, I picked up *Big Giant Floating Head* and studied its cover.

BIG GIANT FLOATING HEAD
A Novel

by

_____ _____

"Excuse me but I just bought that," said the paper man.

I turned the book over and read the back cover. *A stunning lar forcefield*, Big Giant Floating Head *chronicles the author's sharp descent in a world too strange and lonely for him to navigate. Just when he thinks he can't lose any more, language itself breaks down on him. In the stunning finale, _____ can't even utter his ex-wife's name.*

"What?" I said out loud.

"What," said What.

I thumbed through the pages. There was my story about dropping out of school; here was the story about the Lipolian—

"Sir," said the paper man.

—and here was "DivorceLand" and "The Unloveables." And all of them attributed to _____!

Then the paper man snatched the book out of my hand. "Thank you very much," he sang, and he spun on his heels and strode away from the counter.

"Wait," I said, and I followed him out the door, where he stopped by a paper-thin scooter. "Excuse me?" I said.

He turned to face me.

"I—," I said. "I need that book."

"Which one?"

"The floating head one."

"Well you can't have it," said the paper man. "We're reading this in my book club."

"No no," I said. "What I mean is, that book is mine."

"It most certainly is *not*," he said, mounting the scooter. "You just saw me pay for it! Go check with the owner, maybe she has another copy."

"I need that copy too, though," I said. "I need every copy."

The paper man started up the scooter. "Buddy, I don't know what it is today? But I'm in a fucking shitty mood—I have zero tolerance for this right now."

"Those are *my* failures," I said. "*My* walls."

"Well, I look forward to reading about them," he said. Then he drove away, taking my life—years of my life!—with him.

HOTEL

The hotel held everyone I'd ever known: my father, my mother, my brother, ex-girlfriends, friends from way back, near-strangers I'd met briefly and never seen again, even enemies. It was called the Tetherly Inn, and I chose it at random for a sales trip that would take us—my co-worker Mal and me—to Pittsburgh for two nights. At my boss Cheryl's suggestion I'd lined up the hotel on one of those aggregate websites where you don't see the name of the place until after you book the room. The Tetherly was close to the factory we were visiting, though, and it was within our price range, and the ratings were good. "I like to think of the Tetherly as my home away from home," said one review. "They treated us like family!" said another.

We landed in Pittsburgh in the early evening and took a cab to the Tetherly. As soon as we walked in, though, I froze by the fountain in the lobby and Mal almost crashed into me. "Whoa," she said. "You OK?"

"Yeah. Just, this place looks so much like—"

"Like what?"

"Like—my *basement*," I said.

Mal scrunched up her face. "Does your basement *smell* this bad?"

"In the home where I grew up, I mean," I said. "Back in Massachusetts." Save for the fountain, this place *was* my basement: I recognized my old posters of Pink Floyd and Rush stapled to the drop ceiling, a 386Mhz computer hooving away on a rolltop desk like my dad's, a signed Marty Barrett Frisbee on the wall, an easel and a record player in the corner. It had the same dim lighting and that same air of mildew.

"Let's check in, hah?" Mal said. "I'm starving."

We approached the desk and a woman who was the spit and image of my grandmother looked up from her computer and said, "Good evening. Checking in or checking out?"

I was so surprised I couldn't speak. Not only was it my *grand-mère*—who I hadn't seen in twenty years—but she spoke perfect English.

"Arriving," you said.

"Well, welcome to the Tetherly," my grandmother said. "Let's get you squared away. Can I see a driver's license?"

I handed her my license, thinking that she'd recognize me, but she scanned it and handed it back to me. Then she checked the screen and said, "I'll just get your keycards, OK?"

"What *is* this place?" I whispered to Mal.

"Relax, alright?" she said. "It's only a crappy motel."

"Excuse me," said another man behind the counter. "Are you being helped?" I'd met this guy only once before in my life, but I'd never forget him. Ten years earlier, maybe, we got into an altercation at a traffic circle after I cut him off in my pickup. He got out of his Jeep and started shouting at me, his chest puffed out and his face absolutely purple. I said something snide—"It's called a blinker, you should try it sometime"—and his fist came down and smashed me to the ground.

"We're all set," Mal told him now.

"Great," he said.

Then my grandmother whirred back into the room with two cards. "Here we are," she said. "Missus Roy is in room five seven seven—"

An alarm went off in my mind. I said, "Could I—"

"—and Mr. Bowcher is in five sixteen B."

"No no no," said a thought in my mind—I already knew from the numbers what we'd find in those rooms. My grandmother placed the keycards on the counter. I said, "Would it be possible for us to switch?"

"What?" said Mal. "Why?"

My grandmother furrowed her brow. "Switch rooms?"

"That *she* could have five sixteen and—"

"What's the *difference*?" Mal said, looking perturbed.

"Whatever you prefer," said my grandmother. "It'll just take me a minute to—"

"That's OK—these rooms are fine," said Mal, and she took the keycard for 577. I didn't want to cause trouble—especially not for my poor grandmother—so I took the other keycard and picked up my luggage.

We rode the elevator—the same elevator I had in my dorm at Carnegie Mellon, which always smelled a little like vomit— up to the third floor, and I walked the hallway of my high school (blue chalky wall tile) down to my room. Just as I'd thought, I opened the door to find a dimly lit hospital room— the room my father was in for weeks following emergency surgery. Before I even pulled back the curtain I recognized the smell—a mix of lotion, latex, and blood. Then I saw my father circa 1985—the year before he disappeared on us—strapped to the bed, struggling mildly against his wrist restraints, the monitor next to him beeping softly every now and again.

Just being back there made me want to cry. I stood at the foot of the bed, feeling that same panicky dread—*Wake up. Wake up. WAKE UP.*—and then I calmed down and remembered where—when—I was.

The adjacent bed was empty so I lay down in it. My dad stirred. I found my cellphone and called my wife ██. I didn't know if she would answer, but she did. "What," she said.

"I'm sorry," I said, "I know I'm—"

"You're not supposed to be calling me."

"I know," I said. "I know I'm not."

"That's the whole *point* of a separation—to live *separate* lives."

"Can I just tell you what's going on here?"

"Oh, sure," ██ said sarcastically. "What's *going on there*, Chris?"

"I'm in Pittsburgh tonight? At some sort of strange—hotel of my past," I said. "My grandmother's here, and my brother, and multiple versions of my father, I think, and I'm sure you're probably here somewhere, too."

"Uh huh," said ██. "Wow. Wild."

"I'm telling you the truth," I said.

"It sounds like one of your stories."

"It isn't," I said. "It's happening right now!"

"You always do this, Chris," ██ said. "You let your imagination get the best of you, confuse what could happen with what's really happening."

"██? I swear to God I'm lying next to—"

"Hold on," said ██. Then she covered up the receiver and I heard two muffled voices.

"Is someone there?" I said.

"OK—I'm back," she said.

"Who's there?"

"No one. Finish what you were saying."

"Just tell me," I said.

"Am I not allowed to have people over, Chris?" she said. "You can go on a trip with another woman—"

"What? Who, Mal?"

"—who I'm sure you're telling all your stories in *great detail*—"

"That's not true at all!" I said.

"—and I can't host a few friends for dinner? Jesus!" Then she hung up the phone.

My mind swung its fists. I called her back, but she didn't pick up—the phone went right to message. "Mal is not *another woman*," I told the beep. "This is a business trip. You know Cheryl likes to pair a writer and a reader—the client gets a kick out of it.

"Listen—we're supposed to be working on things, aren't we? Maybe when I get home we could get together. For fun, I mean. Like a date. Would you like to go on a date with me? Call me back."

I hung up the phone, lay back in the hospital bed, waited a minute, and then called again. When the call went to voicemail I said, "It's really frustrating when I can't reach you. What if it were an emergency? It *is* an emergency, sort of! Please call me back. Please! Call me back."

I hung up. A minute or two later, ■ texted me. *Can't talk right now. No thanks to the date. Sorry.*

My heart flipped over in its cage. A wave of heat ran over

me. I picked up the hotel phone and called Mal's room. "Hello?" she said breathlessly.

"Hey," I said. "Do you mind if I come over? My room—"

"I was just about to take a shower," she said.

My mind stammered. "I thought we could go over the presentation," I said.

"We've gone over it and over it."

"Cheryl will freak if we don't have our shit together," I said.

Mal exhaled. "Give me an hour, OK?"

I found a laminated menu on the table between the hospital beds, and, inside, a list of all the foods from my childhood: grilled water rolls, potato chips, soda, pizza, spaghetti, pizza rolls, and what my dad used to call "American Chop Suey"—elbow macaroni with ground beef and sauce. I ordered up some of that and a half an hour later there was a knock on the door. I opened it to see my dad circa 1983 standing there with two plastic microwave bowls. "Hey bud," he said, and he stepped past me into the room. "Hothothot!" He rushed past himself in the hospital bed and put the bowls down on the table. "Zapped it too long," he said. He didn't ask if he could eat with me—he just found a chair and pushed a plate at me. *"Mange, mange!"* he said, and we dove at the food just like we used to, wolfing down the cheap ground chuck and the discount noodles. We heard the crack of a bat on the TV screen, saw the ball go over the Green Monster and Bob Stanley hang his head in despair. "He crushed that thing," I said.

"They're bums!" my dad said, ripping open a bag of Lay's. We polished off the bag in about ten minutes.

Then the phone rang—it was Mal. "Coming over?" she said.

"Yeah," I said. "I'll be right there."

My dad licked the salt off his fingers. "I'll let you go," he said. He hopped off the bed, looked at his unconscious self, and then disappeared into the hall. I tried to follow him, but he stepped into the stairwell—I heard the fire door slam behind him.

I turned and walked in the other direction, toward Mal's room. On the way, I passed my cousin Andre—who was paralyzed in a construction accident when I was nineteen—walking with his wife Lynn. I stopped and watched him strut. When he stepped into an elevator I knocked on Mal's door; she appeared with her hair wet and curly. "Hey," she said.

"Holy *shit*," I said, looking over her shoulder.

"What?" she said.

"This *room*. This is my old *room!*"

It was: there was my single bed with the Superman bed sheets, my dresser with my Roger Clemens rookie card on top, my black and gold R.E.M. shirt lumped in the corner near the window. "That's my desk!" I said. "Where I started writing! And holy shit, my old tube amp!"

"You seriously lived here?"

"For about ten years," I said.

"Maybe you know what this is, then," Mal said, tossing me a small plastic box.

I recognized it before I even caught it: it was a Tic-Tac box with a drawing of a number pad stuffed inside. "This was my pretend remote," I said. "I haven't seen this thing in twenty-five years. See the numbers?"

"What's the point of it, though? It doesn't do anything."

"All of my friends had TVs with remotes in their room," I said, "and I just had this black-and-white. So I made my own remote."

She shook her head.

I opened up the dresser: There were my clothes—stone-washed jeans and high tube socks and Izod shirts—all of them reeking of my mother's cigarettes.

Mal sat down at my desk with the presentation packet. "Want to go over this?" she said.

"Give me just a second." I went over to my bookshelf and thumbed through the rows of tag sale paperbacks: old coughed copies of *The Boy No One Could Hear, A Very Bad Smell, You Will Always Be Alone.* "These books were my *friends*," I said.

Eventually, Mal stood up from my desk and announced that she was going out to see the city. I stayed behind; I spent the whole evening in that room, going through the old drawers of my life. I'd saved so much *junk* over the years: souvenirs from trips to New York City and D.C.; old floppy disks; every comic book and magazine I'd ever owned. I read old letters from girlfriends and pen pals, and remembered the friends I'd had and lost: a kid I'd met in D.C. who turned out to be a kleptomaniac; the girlfriend I'd had in Maine, whose father let us drink. Here was a book I'd made by stapling each dot-matrix–printed page into a composition notebook; here was the journal I'd kept during a semester in Europe. Inside that journal, I found a drawing of St. Paul's cathedral. (God, if I could actually find that journal now. Not in one of my novels, I mean, but in real life. I'd give anything for it.) Those drawers seemed to hold everything. As I dug deeper I found sand from a beach in Nice; a still-living sunfish from Lake Congamond; my grandfather's BB gun. I pulled them all out onto the carpet and reached my arm in farther.

What was I looking for? It wasn't just the past. I was looking for *me*—the me that had lived here in this house, in this life, and grown up to become the guy █ fell in love with. I'd lost that person somewhere, traded him for a traveling word salesman, a writer of stories and nothing else. I think that was why I found the Tetherly when I did. If that hotel still held my past, I thought it might know my future, too.

Mal came back around one in the morning, tipsy and smelling of sweat. She brushed her teeth, put on her pajamas, and hinted that she was tired. I was showing her a ribbon that I'd won at a swim meet when she clapped her hands and said, "OK Chris. Out."

Just then, though, I pulled an old yellowed rope bracelet from the back of the drawer. "God," I said. "My mom would buy us these every year when we went to Cape Cod. I probably got this when I was ten or eleven—"

"Chris? I have to get to sleep." Mal pointed to the door. "Out. Right now."

I gathered up what I could—the Europe journal, the baseball card, a few letters, the sand—and took it back to the hospital room. When I opened the door my father stirred. "*Maman?*" he said.

"It's OK, Dad," I said.

I was up most of the night reading the letters and the journal. Nurses came in every hour to check on my father, and once, around four a.m., they wheeled him out for tests. In the morning, I opened my eyes to find my mother circa 1981 sitting by my father's bed and reading a thick hardcover library book.

"Mom?" I said.

She looked over at me, smiled, and continued reading.

"█ and I are getting divorced," I said.

She didn't respond—it was, true to my childhood, as if I'd said nothing at all.

"She's not sure she loves me anymore," I said.

My mother flipped the page in her book.

When I met Mal downstairs the next morning, she snorted and said, "Christ—you look awful. Didn't you sleep?"

We drove a rental car to the fiction factory—Pittsburgh Fiction—where we were supposed to meet with the acquisitions guy, Roland Ferris, and present him with the most robust, expensive package of adjectives sold by my company, Descriptor, Inc. A one-year lease on these adjectives would pay out upwards of a million dollars—that was the whole reason for this junket.

But when I shook Ferris's hand, I saw clouds in his eyes and I could tell that something was wrong. He led us into a meeting room and we began our pitch. We'd actually taken some of his factory's products—excerpts from their novels *Manatee* and *Alabama Mort*—and revised them, just to illustrate how spry they'd read with our adjectives. Not five minutes in, though, Ferris held up his hands and said, "Let me stop you for a second here. This package is impressive, but the board held a meeting last week and they decided—" he took a breath, "—against description."

Mal and I looked at each other. "I'm sorry?" she said.

"You're staying with your current description package, you mean," I said.

Ferris shook his head. "Our new line of novels? No description, period."

I was totally thrown. "But how—"

"The trustees think adjectives are—expendable. Unnecessary. 'Useless bloat,' one of them said."

Mal stood up. "Now wait a second," she said. "Adjectives are *not* useless—"

"Why didn't anyone tell us this?" I said. "Before we came all this way!"

"I was hoping I could change their minds! I thought maybe if they *saw* the new adjectives at work—"

"Because readers and writers agree," I said, gesturing toward Mal and then myself, "that this is one of the most exciting collections of adjectives in the modern description era."

"I'm sorry," said Ferris, "but I just can't move the needle at these prices."

As the cab carried us back to our hotel, I called Cheryl on my cell. "What do you mean, *no description?*" she shouted.

"That's what Ferris said," I told her.

"You're fucking with me," she said.

"I'm not," I said.

"I mean, he told me they were restructuring, but nothing about this! How are they going to write a single scene?"

"I know—it's insane," I said.

Cheryl took a breath. "Let me just take a second, figure out what to do here."

The cab turned into the lot for the Tetherly. I was anxious to get back to the artifacts in my room.

"Chris?" said Cheryl.

"I'm here," I said.

"Listen. I'm going to change the itinerary, send you on—" I heard the clicking of keys. "—to Phoenix."

"Right from here?"

"You'll fly out today, meet with—"

"Today," I repeated.

"There's a flight that leaves this afternoon at—"

"Any chance it can be tomorrow instead?" I said.

"I need you to meet with the Bersons first thing tomorrow, see if we can't move some of these adjectives after all."

My heart sank. "I'll tell Mal," I said.

"Actually, I'm keeping her there to meet with our Pittsburgh distributor—they've got an office in Squirrel Hill. Tell her I'll text her the deets."

"Oh," Mal said when I told her. "Huh." We walked into the hotel and rode the elevator up to the fifth floor. Back in my room, I found my father writhing in pain. I sat down in the chair next to him and adjusted his pillow. Then I sent a text to Cheryl: *Any chance I could take a few days' vacation?*

Now!? she replied. *Please, C. Lets get thru this clusterfuck and then well find a time to give u a break. OK?*

I had less than half an hour to pack; I stuffed the journal and a few letters into my suitcase and left everything else behind. When I got down to the lobby, my mother circa 1993 was standing on a stepladder and fixing a light bulb. "Mom?"

She looked down at me.

"I've got to go," I said.

"*Welche?*" she said.

This mother, I realized, was another version altogether. "I'll come back, OK?" I said.

She stared at me blankly.

I murdled past her and over to the front desk. A friend of

mine from childhood—a kid named Del, who walked with a
limp and always smelled like cats—was standing at one of the
terminals. "Can I help you?" he said.

"Is my *father* available, by any chance?" I asked.

"Your—I'm sorry?" he said.

"My dad?" I said. "He delivered my dinner last night, to
room—"

I will always love you

"Let me see if I can find out who was working in the kitchen
last night." He typed some information into the computer, and
then scrunched up his face. "I'm sorry—I don't know who
you're referring to."

I had to get going if I was going to catch my flight. I took
one last look around—there, in a dark corner, was my cassette
shelf on the wall! The Jethro Tull tapes I never returned to the
library!—and I lifted the handle of my suitcase and walked out
through the glass doors.

It wasn't until later—on the plane, in fact, flying west over
the middle pages—that I realized what had happened. That
Mal wasn't just any character, but one from my distant past.
That name, Mal, lived way back in my mind; it was short for
Malvina, the name of my father's grandmother. "Mal" belonged
there. But why didn't I?

I went on to live other lives: lives in Arizona, Anchor-
age, Buffalo, Stein, Montreal, Ann Arbor. I sold adjectives—
newfangled adjectives, antique adjectives—all over the world. I
made a lot of money.

All the while, though, Mal remained in my past. Shortly
after our stay at the Tetherly, she became Descriptor's chief liai-
son to the Pittsburgh distributor. When the distributor bought

a portion of the company, she relocated. And she stayed at the Tetherly so often during those transitional months that she became part of the place; everyone knew her there. She lived *my* life: She swam on the swim team and graduated from Coolidge High School; she worked at the Coolidge Summer Theater and studied in Norwich, England.

Sometimes, late at night, I'd call Mal from the road. She wouldn't usually answer, but one time she did. "Hello?" she said.

"Hey."

"Oh, hey," she said.

"What's happening there?"

"Your brother's watching television and eating cucumbers and salad dressing," she said.

"That's what he ate every night for years," I said.

There was a moment of awkward silence. Then she said, "This life is still here for you, Chris. OK? Trust me—these stories aren't going anywhere."

But that wasn't true. Seven months later, Cheryl finally gave me a long-overdue vacation and I flew back to Pittsburgh. When I called the Tetherly, though, there weren't any vacancies—not for the week of my vacation nor the week before or after. I decided to go there anyways to see if there might be a cancellation. This was right after my divorce, one of the loneliest and most difficult times I've known so far, and I needed the Tetherly—my friends and family, in whatever version they were available—more than ever.

When I checked at the front desk, though, my grandmother read the screen and said, "I'm sorry, sir. We're all booked."

"How about for tomorrow night?"

"Sheesh," she said, mock-wincing. "We don't have a vacancy all this week."

I thanked her and sat down in the lobby; the chairs were the puffy corduroy recliners from my parents' living room. I stayed there for about half an hour. At one point, our dead chihuahua came over, sniffed my foot—"Herman!" I said—growled at me and moved on. As I watched the people from my life brisk to and from the front desk, I started studying their patterns. Twice, my grandmother walked into a door right behind the desk. When the door opened, I caught a glimpse inside that back room: I saw a man with glasses—my old friend Neal! We took guitar lessons from the same teacher—looking at a computer monitor, and behind him, a giant illuminated picture of my father's old orange leather coat—the one he let me borrow once for a high school dance.

After about ten minutes, an influx of visitors—my friend Drew, who died on my nineteenth birthday; a woman I recognized but couldn't place; the wife of the pastor of my church—all lined up to check in at the same time. While my grandmother and the bully scrambled to accommodate them, I leapt up from the chair, walked around the front desk, and tried the door to the back room. The knob turned; I slipped into the room and quietly closed the door behind me.

Inside that room, four or five people—Neal, my father's friend Murphy, others I didn't recognize—sat at screens with their backs turned to me. Each wall, meanwhile, was covered with projections of images from my life—experiences and memories layered one over the other. There was the night I met

; the green bicycle hat, covered with pins, that I wore when I was ten; my high school drama teacher. On the other wall I saw my ex-girlfriend Molly; the leather Eastman shoes I wore in the fifth grade; the moment when Melody and I were sitting in Coolidge Grinders and she asked me to marry her.

I stood there silently for a minute or two, watching the images change. What *was* this? How did they get all this information?

Next to me, I noticed now, was a food-service cart with a full loaf of bread—my grandmother's bread, which would crumble when you picked it up—with a jar of *cretons* from my Aunt Jeannine's kitchen table.

I couldn't help myself—I reached for a slice of bread. But it was fresh out of the oven, and too hot—I hissed and put it down. When I did, Neal turned around. His eyes went wide and he shouted "Hey!" The woman next to him picked up a phone. My grandmother stormed into the room and put a strong hand on my shoulder. "Sir," she said. "You're not supposed to be in here. Let's go. Now."

"Please," I said. "Tell me what all of this is supposed to be."

Then two security guards—my mother and father, dressed in blue uniforms—rushed in and took hold of my arms. "This is private property, sir, and you are trespassing," said my father through gritted teeth. They pulled me out of the control room and through the lobby.

"Mom," I said, weeping. "Mommy."

My parents walked me past the elevator and the front desk and out through the front door. Then they shoved me onto the semi-circle driveway. When I turned around to protest, my mother unclipped a taser from her belt. "Vacate the premises immediately," she said, "or we'll restrain you and call the police."

"OK," I said, "OK." I stumbled over to my rental car by the side of the building. By then it was dark. When I sat down in the driver's seat I could see, through the giant glass windows, the hotel's dining room—which was identical, of course, to the one in my parents' house. Everyone in the hotel—my parents, my grandparents, the bully, my pastor, my ex-wife and ex-girlfriends—was sitting down around a giant table that held endless plates of food: turkeys and hams and roasts and salads and cheeses and breads and cakes and pies. Mal was there, too—she saw me through the glass and waved at me contritely. To her right, my father said something to my brother, and my brother threw his head back and laughed. What was so funny? I'd never know.

That place. Those people. I sat there for a minute or two watching them. Then I drove out of my life and I never went back.

PARADE

Halfway through the divorce proceedings we heard a noise outside—marching, shouting, clapping—and we ran to the window to investigate. People lined the sidewalks—a father carried his son on his shoulders and a few elderly people sat in lawn chairs and pointed toward the intersection.

My lawyer peered down the street. "Is it a protest?"

Then we all saw what it was.

"It's a parade," ███ said.

The four of us went outside. Soon, the procession started passing by. It was led by our parents—███'s mother, my deceased father—who carried a banner that displayed my name and ███'s. It read, "Married: July 10, 2010. Divorced:," and today's date. My dead father shot me a look of disapproval as he marched by.

They were followed by a marching band—fifteen or twenty musicians in red uniforms. "Who are these people?" I yelled to ███.

She pointed to the bass drum, which read "The Lonely Morning Marching Band."

"The Lonely Morning Marching Band!" she shouted.

Then ███'s grandfather came by in an antique Ford. The onlookers clapped for him. "Grandpa!" yelled ███. "What the hell are you doing?"

"Your mother's idea!" he said.

████'s brother Leo and his wife followed in a horse 'n' buggy—Leo gave me the finger before his wife pulled his arm down.

The I Don't Love You Players were next, followed by a series of floats depicting scenes from our marriage. The first showed a miniature, sagging version of our house made of chicken wire and cardboard. Then came the Full of Regret Orchestra and a float carrying a woman that looked like my new girlfriend, Ingrid. She stood outside a papier-mâché motel in lingerie and waved regally to the crowd. A guy across the street put his fingers to his mouth and whistled at her.

Then the parade was over. As soon as the last float passed by the crowd dispersed. Our lawyers walked back inside and we turned to follow. I held the door open for ██ and she smiled coyly as she passed by. "We were more than just a bunch of *floats*, Chris," she said.

"I know it."

"Let's just get through this, OK?"

I nodded and she walked inside. But I didn't follow—I let the door close.

By now the street was empty—everyone had gone back to their lives. I walked into the middle of the road, and a man came by carrying bags of cotton candy on sticks. I bought one from him and unwrapped it. It was as big as my head.

██ came back outside. "Chris?" she said.

I leaned into the web of pink sweetness, and stuck out my tongue.

THE UNLOVEABLES

Two days after my wife leaves there's a knock on the door. It's an Unloveable. He's got a crisp white shirt on, a backpack over his shoulder and a folder in his hand. "Good afternoon, Mr. Boucher," he says. "We are very sorry to hear about your divorce."

"It's a separation," I say. "Look, I told you last month—"

"But things are different now, Mr. Boucher," he says. "Love has failed you. Your adoration score has never been lower."

I try not to look at the hole in the man's chest.

"Listen," he says, and he holds up a tablet and points to a three-dimensional, multicolored chart. "No one loves you. I can say that with absolute certainty—we have the data right here."

"Maybe not currently," I say. "But that could change."

"The point is, why *chase* love? Why live that way in the first place? Now, I don't know if you know who we are, or what we do—"

"I do," I say.

"Well then you know that we're an international volunteer organization, and one of the single most charitable enterprises on the planet."

"Yes," I say.

"And do you know *why* we're so successful?"

"I think I do," I say.

"Because we're *focused*, Mr. Boucher," says the Unloveable. "Wholly dedicated. And since we're resigned to a life alone, we can direct all that energy—"

"Look, I know all this," I say. "My father was an Unloveable—one of the first."

"He—oh." The Unloveable checks his notes. "He was?"

"But I'm just not interested in joining. OK?" I start to close the door.

"Can I leave you with some literature, at least? Maybe you know someone else who isn't loved, and you can pass it on to them?"

"Sure," I say.

The Unloveable hands me a brochure. "My card's attached, in case you need to reach me," he says.

I nod and thank him. Then I close the door and throw the brochure and card in the recycling bin.

·✦·

In the weeks that follow I do the best I can to rescue my marriage. My wife agrees to meet with a marriage counselor, but she cancels the first session at the last minute and shows up late for the second. Midway through that meeting I turn to face her and say, "I just think, couldn't we go back to the beginning, when we first met, and—"

"That was nine years ago, Chris," says.

"—I know it will take a lot of work," I say. "But I'm prepared for that. I *want* to do that work."

"But I don't," ■ says to me. Then she turns to the therapist. "I don't mean this to be hurtful, but I'm really excited about the next phase, and a life *without* Chris."

We finalize the divorce a few weeks later. By then my wife has moved from the hotel where she was staying to a new condo complex in Blix. Movers arrive one day and load up most of our furniture: the couch, the dining room table, most of the kitchenware, our bed. That same week I start seeing a psychiatrist who tells me that I am grieving. "What you're going through is like a death," he says.

"That's exactly how it feels," I say. "Like death. I feel dead. I am *dead*."

"*You're* not dead," says the psychiatrist. "But you're recovering from a significant loss. And that'll take time."

Even though he advises against it, I create a profile on old andsingle.com and start going on dates. The first one is with a woman named Katharyn; she's the town clerk in East Geryk. Over dinner at The Question Mark she asks me what I do for a living. "I'm a fiction writer," I say.

"Oh?" she says. "What kind of fiction?"

"Experimental novels, mostly," I say.

"I mean what *type*," she says, smiling—she has a wide, beautiful smile. "Horror novels? Mysteries?"

"Not really either of those," I say.

And I'll never stop missing you

"Well I'd love to read something you've written," she says.

I email her a floating head called "Lady with Invisible Dog." She writes back, "Thanks so much for showing this to me! It's so imaginative!" But that's all the email says. I email her back to thank her and ask her out again, but she never replies.

A few weeks later I go out with a woman named Belinda. She's getting divorced herself, and we meet for tea and commiserate. "It's like, you think your life is going down a certain path," she says. "And then, wham."

"I know it—wham," I say.

"Now everything is different and awful," she says. Then she looks at me over her cup of tea, twists her face up and says, "You're a little balder than I thought."

"Oh," I say. "Well—"

"Your picture doesn't show your hair."

"It's kind of an old picture," I admit.

"My husband had long hair," she says. "Ex. Has. My *ex*-husband *has* long hair. God," she says. She covers her face with her hands and begins to cry. "I'm sorry," she says.

"It's OK," I say.

"It's like why couldn't we have—I mean, he and I never even considered . . ." she trails off. Then she says, "Will you give me just one second?"

"Sure," I say.

"I just need to ask him a question," she says, fishing in her purse.

"Who?" I say.

Belinda finds her phone and dials a number, and I hear a voice on the other end. "Steve?" she says.

I lean back in my chair and look around the café.

"I know," she says. "I know. I just—I wanted to—you were? Me too. Me *too*!" Then she listens for a moment. "I was just thinking that exact same thing! But—I know. We never even talked about that as a possibility. Yes. *Yes.* That's what I was trying to tell you when—right. I want that, too!" He says something, and she says, "Right now, I can come over right now." She stands up and grabs her purse. "OK, honey—I love you, too." She walks out of the café without even looking back at me.

After a few more unsuccessful dates, I cancel my account on oldandsingle. Then, a few months later, I'm talking on the phone with Candice, a new editor at the newspaper I write for, and she suggests we meet to talk about my article on Friday night. I think, Friday night! I'm very flattered; I clean up the house, put on some nice jeans and my black shirt, and make salmon. When Candice shows up at my door she's wearing sweatpants and carrying her laptop. She looks me over and says, "Wait. Did you—aren't we editing?"

"Sure," I say. "Sorry. Yeah. I'll get my laptop."

"Did you think this was a—something else?"

"No. Just that, it's Friday night."

"And the story's due on Monday," Candice says.

"Of course, no problem," I say, my face hot with shame.

When she leaves that night, I close the front door behind her and sit down on the floor of my near-empty house. I don't cry—I just sit there and wait to feel better, for the loneliness to go away. I fall asleep right there on the hardwood, and the next morning I wake up to a knocking—someone's at the door. I stand up and look through the window; it's an Unloveable. When I open the door she says, "Hello. My name is Allie, and I'm something called—" she makes air quotes, "—an Unloveable. I was wondering if I could take a few minutes to tell you about our organization."

"I know about it," I say. "My dad was an Unloveable, one of the first."

"No kidding," she says. She smiles weakly. "Well, then, I don't need to give you the pitch."

"No," I say, chuckling.

"And I bet you don't need a brochure," she says.

"I'll take one, actually, if that's OK."

"Absolutely," she says, and she hands me a brochure. Then she pulls her folder close to her chest, so I can't see the hole where her heart would be, and says, "We just know how much you're struggling, Mr. Boucher. Your loneliness levels are spiking. That's why my advisor said to drop by."

"Is it possible that I'm in a bad place right now, but that I'll get better?"

"That's not what our research suggests," she says. "Your case study indicates that you'll be alone from here on out."

"You don't know that for sure, though," I say.

"Right," she concedes. "But our data models—"

"The future is a mystery, is what I'm saying."

"Sure," the Unloveable says, and shrugs. "Anyways. Be well, Mr. Boucher." Then she turns and walks down the steps and away from the house.

I go to the bathroom and then sit back down on the floor and read the brochure.

Are you tired of feeling unloved? Have you tried dating and failed? Do you feel ugly? The problem isn't you, it's the world around you—a world in which we believe we deserve love. We

challenge you to destroy that myth. Step out of
the rat race—that constant, daily attempt to try
to find people who love you. Face it, no one
will! The people who did love you are dead, or
they've changed their minds! Face facts! Embrace
a life without love! Become an Unloveable!

© Unloveables of America, Inc.

There are also some testimonials ("Love only ever caused
me problems. A life without love is the life for me!"; "I finally
understand what it means to be free."), some Facts About Love
("Love is blind."; "Love is dumb."; "Love is a thief."; "Love's an
illness."), plus pictures of Unloveables volunteering—digging
in the dirt, dishing out soup—and a list of abilities that Unloveables gain: they can eat without gaining weight; they don't get
depressed; they don't need sleep. And then, at the very bottom,
in small type, I see the words "Important: Heart Attacks™ Are
Required for All Unloveables!"

I know most of this already: the heart removals, the
volunteerism, the new abilities—I'd heard about it all
from my father, who left me, my mother, and my brother when
I was eleven. He'd had a triple bypass the year before, and he
decided he wanted to see the world. He took a job tracking
down missing stories; I know he was in the Australian out-
back for a while, and then in Colombia. The rest of my family
shunned him when he left, but I kept in sparse contact with
him: he wrote me a letter when I graduated from high school,
and we met once for lunch the summer after my freshman year
of college. But then I didn't hear from him again until I was
twenty-three, when he called to ask about the Unloveables.

"There's this program," he told me over the phone, "called the Society for People Not Loved by Anyone." (That's what they first called themselves when the program was founded: the SPNLA.)

"Uh huh," I said.

"They take your heart, but I've got a bum ticker anyway," he said. "So I think I'm going to join up."

"OK."

"Unless you tell me right now that I shouldn't."

"I haven't seen you in four years," I said. "What do you expect me to say?"

"It's meant for people who aren't loved by anyone in the whole entire world. Is that me, Chris? Do I fit that bill?"

"Do whatever you want," I said, and I hung up the phone.

About a year later I got an email from my dad, saying he was going to be in town and that maybe he could stop by. We met at the Wandering Cow for coffee. My father had shaved his head—his eyebrows, even—and there was a giant hole in his chest. He ordered two slices of pie and ate them both. "It's so great to see you, Christopher," he said between bites.

"You too," I told him. "Is the Society for People Not Loved—"

"We're called the Unloveables now," he said.

"The Unloveables?"

He nodded.

"Is the program working for you?"

He waved the question away. "Best thing I ever did," he said.

My father was dressed all in white—white shirt, white pants, white socks—but his sneakers were flecked with red. "What's on your shoes?"

But it was like he didn't hear me. "It just feels so good to be *free*," he said. "I've spent the last few weeks volunteering at a home for the elderly out near Utica. And I've met some of the nicest people." Then he held out a forkful of pie. "Pie?"

"No," I said.

My dad cleaned his plate. Then a wash of light passed over his face, and he dropped his fork, stood up next to the table and started bouncing in place.

"Dad," I said.

"What?" he said.

"What are you doing?"

"I don't know." I could hear the wind whistling through his chest. "Dancing, I guess," he said.

"There's no music," I said.

"I know it," he said. "I know there isn't."

That was the last time I saw him. He immersed himself in volunteerism, was never loved again by anyone, and died two years later in a plane crash; he was flying with seven other Unloveables when their tiny plane went down in a field outside of Lawrence, Kansas.

I sit there on the floor that morning and read through the brochure. Then I get my laptop and log onto the Unloveables' website. There's a meeting of the local chapter next Tuesday. I think, Why not? What's the harm? Maybe I'll meet someone there!

The meeting is held in a giant warehouse near the airport. When I approach the door I'm greeted by a burly man with a hole in his chest. "Evening," he says. "Name?"

"I'm just here to learn," I say.

"I still need your name," he says.

"Christopher Boucher," I say.

"Boucher," he says. "Email?"

"Bowcher Booshay at G-mail dot com," I say.

He writes it down. "OK," he says. "Be free."

"Thanks," I say.

I sit down toward the back. There's a low stage in the front of the room with a foldable table on it. There's something on the table, but I can't see what. Soon a woman with very long gray hair takes the stage. "Good evening," she says.

"Good evening," says the audience.

She holds out her hands. "Why are we here?" We stare back at her; no one says anything. "Why?" she says again.

A bald man in the front raises his hand.

"Don't need to raise your hand," she says. "We're not in school."

"Because no one loves us," says the man.

"OK," she says.

"Because we're lonely," says an old woman behind me.

"And we want better lives," says a guy to my right.

"We are here," says the long-haired woman, "because we understand that *love is a lie*. That it's not real. We've seen it. Each and every one of you *know* it at your core. We know that our hearts?" Then she picks up the object on the table. My stomach flips; she's holding a human heart. "Are defects," she says. "Hindrances. That to remove them, to accept the truth about love, allows us to get on with our lives. To maybe even do something great with them." Then she drops the heart back on the table; it lands with a plop. "You are here, ladies and gentlemen, because you're smart. Savvy. Ahead of the curve."

A woman in front of me—she's maybe thirty—coughs.

"Now I'm not going to try and convince you to become an Unloveable, to adopt our codes. I'm not selling anything here. But I will say this." I notice that her white shoes are flecked with pink—just like my dad's. "You wouldn't be here if you didn't already know, in that space in your chest, that love is a lie. If you weren't *already* an Unloveable. The only question to ask yourself is, are you going to accept that fact and change your life? Or will you continue to live the lie?"

Afterward, a line of people forms at the sign-up kiosk. Next to the booth is a machine with a giant metal claw sticking out of it—"HeartAttack 2170," it says on the side. I can hear the *thunk* as the HeartAttack reaches into chests and takes out hearts. *Thunk. Thunk.*

I'm sitting in my seat, watching the line crawl forward, when the burly greeter sits down in the chair behind me, leans forward, and says, "What do you think, friend?"

I turn back to him. "She's a really good speaker."

"We're all good speakers," he says. "Know why? No heart, no adrenaline. No anxiety, either. Also, none of us need sleep."

"So you don't ever sleep," I say, incredulously.

"We sleep for fun," says the greeter, "but not out of necessity."

"Do you ever feel *sad*?" I ask him. "Or lonely?"

"'Course I do," he says. "That's the work. To study the sadness. To see what it really is—and how, at its core, it's empty."

"I'd like to be able to do that. To see my sadness as empty."

"Of course you would," he says, putting a hand on my shoulder. "So what do you say?"

My mind races. "OK," I blurt.

"Yeah?" he says.

"Yes," I say.

"Good man," he says, clapping me on the back. Then I join the line, where I wait for about a half an hour. When I get to the front, the man in the kiosk asks my name, age, and social security number. Then he asks my occupation. "Writer," I say.

"Of?"

"Novels, mostly. Some journalism."

He records my scores for loneliness (98), sorrow (97), and compassion (21). Then he says, "Now, you do understand that you're committing to a life without love."

"Yes," I say.

"And you have no misgivings about doing so?"

"None," I say.

"Sign here," he says.

I sign.

Then, before I even realize what's happening, the claw of the Heart Attacker shoots out and snatches my heart from my chest. It doesn't hurt, but I suddenly feel colder. Also, my vision gets a bit dimmer and my mind flattens. Meanwhile, the machine grinds and burps. Then it goes quiet.

"What happens to the hearts?" I ask the Unloveable.

"Oh, you'll see," he says, smirking. "Next!"

I'm ushered through the warehouse, out the door, and onto a bus. I don't see my house again—I trade it for a bunk bed in a colony of Unloveables, where I'm soon sent on my first assignment: recording testimony and stories from those who have lost their homes to recent fires in the Pacific Northwest. I'm flown out to the high desert where, one by one, the victims of the fires show me what they've lost. "This was my father's home," one woman tells me as we stand in the ruins. "Everything I had left of him was in there. His ashes, even."

"I am sorry," I say, as instructed.

"And, where did it go? Someone *tell* me where my house went."

"I apologize," I say.

She starts to cry.

"Do not cry," I suggest.

One guy, in his early thirties, is in the midst of telling me about his missing dog when he looks down at the hole in my chest and says, "Does it hurt?"

"What?"

"When they take it out," he says.

I shake my head. "You don't feel a thing," I say. Which is true—I don't.

"Because no one loves me either," he says.

"No?" I say. "How about your parents?"

He shakes his head. "Not even my girlfriend. Just Stewart, and I'm pretty sure he's dead."

"Stewart?" I say.

"My lhasa apso," he says.

"I have a brochure if you'd like one," I say.

"I would."

So I give him two brochures—the one they gave me, and another one called *What Will Happen to My Heart?*

It's a common misperception that Unloveables thoughtlessly discard their hearts. This couldn't be further from the truth! In fact, one might say that each colony is powered by hearts. All extracted hearts are brought to the Heartgroves™, where they're respectfully buried in the ground—and where their natural decomposition can fuel the soil with nutrients and new life.

About the Heartgroves™

The name says it all! The Heartgroves™ are dedicated farms that store Unloveables' extracted, buried hearts. Unloveables take responsibility for the management and upkeep of these fields, including heart burials, heartree removal, and blood irrigation.

All of which is true: each of us is required to work ten hours a week in the Heartgroves™. Most of the time I'm assigned to the Burial team, digging trenches in the blood-red ground, but once or twice I help pull down the heartrees—the trees with tiny hearts hanging from the branches that grow when the buried hearts pollinate. Then we all get back on the bus, drive back to our dorms, and scrub the blood off our shoes.

As the weeks pass, I believe I'm making progress—I'm good at collecting testimony, it turns out, and I hardly ever think about being unloved anymore. Plus, my monthly checkups show an improvement in my scores: my loneliness drops to 44 and my sorrow to 51, while my compassion rockets to 62.

One day that fall, though, Master Elvin holds a special

meeting in the auditorium for all of the new recruits. It's clear from his expression that he's not pleased. "I look around here," he says, standing at the edge of the stage, "and I don't see proud, stable Unloveables. I see rookies—deluded, self-congratulatory, hardly unloveable at all. You think you've accomplished something, right? You're living in the colony, working a steady job, helping others. You think you see the lie, am I right?"

Some of the older Unloveables in the back chuckle.

"But the truth is, you haven't really done anything yet—not really. You're a first-level Unloveable. Meaning, you're only working at not being loved. Fine. But the true work here? Is not only to accept that you are not loved, but to realize that *you don't love anyone*. That you never have. That you never will. How could you," Master Elvin says, smiling wryly, "if love *itself* is a lie?"

I feel an echo in my chest—the memory of a pang.

Then Elvin studies his shoes, paces across the stage, and looks back up at the crowd. "Today, I'd like to talk to you about an advanced Unloveables' practice called 'Non-loving Kindness.' Its essence is, you can be kind to someone without even liking them. Watch." Then he calls on an Unloveable— it's Garvey, I know him—and Garvey stands up in his chair. "How are you today, Garvey?" says Master Elvin.

"Fine," says Garvey.

"Great, that's really great," says Master Elvin, smiling brightly. Then he turns to us. "See, I don't really care at all how Garvey's doing. I could give a shit. But does he know that?"

"I do now," says Garvey, and everyone laughs.

I try to internalize this—to resist loving anything—but I'm not sure how to do it. So I go see Master Elvin during his office hours. "What you were talking about a few days ago," I ask him, "Non-loving—"

"Non-loving Kindness," he says. "What about it?"

"I want to know how to do that. Is it the same as *hating* everything, or . . . ?"

Master Elvin smiles. "Consider the premise of your question, Christopher. You don't *do* it and get it *done*. Non-loving Kindness is a practice. It takes constant vigilance." As he's talking, I notice something: I can tell from the shape of his robe that there's no hole in his chest. It must have closed—which I've heard can happen to the extremely devout. "For example," he says, "what do you love about this room you're in right now?"

I look around his office. "Not anything, I don't think."

"Do you love the idea of attention? Attention from me?"

"Oh." I think about that.

"What about the idea of improvement—do you love that?"

"That's a good question," I say.

"Non-loving Kindness is like—like wearing a special pair of glasses. When you look through them, everything is different. The practice should inform every single moment of your life."

In the weeks that follow, I do my best to cultivate a Non-loving Kindness practice. When I'm promoted from Story Collector to Assistant Editor in the Office of Brochures soon afterward, for example, I try not to be too proud of myself—to love, or even like, myself. I make a few new friends at the Brochure Office—my editor, Koyalee; a designer named Stan—but

I make sure they're not good friends. If they try to strike up a conversation, I stifle it. When they invite me to eat lunch with them, I decline.

Soon I am on the path to Non-loving Kindness, which is to say: I no longer regard anything as beautiful. Nothing is awful, though, either. Everything just *is*. The Heartgroves™, the checkups, the scrubbing of blood off of my shoes—it's all basically the same unremarkable, unspecial, unloveable moment. In fact, I could use any word to describe it: "garden," "rope," "odyssey," "driveway." My friends are driveway. My dorm is driveway. Our brochures are driveway. Eventually the walls of my hearthole harden and the hole starts to reduce in size. I still miss my heart from time to time—"ghost pangs," Master Elvin calls those—but by Thanksgiving my hearthole is a pinhole; it barely lets the light through.

That winter, though, disaster strikes close to home when a terrible worrying plague hits western Massachusetts. People are struck, quite suddenly, by such crippling worries that they can't leave their homes. The Unloveables mobilize and go door-to-door, trying to assuage the worries of anyone reporting sudden anxiety. I'm called out of the Brochure Office to help in the field—to go door-to-door in Blix. Late in my third day of canvasing, I knock on a door and, to my complete surprise, my ex-wife ▉ answers. "Chris?" she says.

I search my list. All it shows is the last name: it's ▉▉▉▉▉.
"▉?" I say.

She slams the door closed.

"Wait!" I knock on the door. "I'm here to help, ▉! Please. Just to help with the anxiety."

She opens the door and lets me in. Her house smells like urine. "Tell me about your anxiety, ███," I say.

"What are you doing here?" she says.

"I'm an Unloveable," I say, cheerfully. "My list says that someone named ████████ lives here."

"That's my husband, ████ █████████," she says, her face a dark sky. Then I can see her looking me over. "Is this my fault, Chris? Did you join this cult because of me?"

"It's not a cult, ███," I say. "And it's no one's fault."

Her eyes start to shimmer. Then she says, "Remember the green house, Chris?"

"Not really," I say.

"Where we'd sit out on the back deck? And remember that flat we lived in—the coffin?"

"Sort of," I admit.

"What—" I can see her mind twisting. "What *happens* to those moments?"

"We sold most of them," I point out.

"No, I mean, everything. Our lives. What do we do with it?"

"My teacher says we turn it all into stories," I say. "That helps us detach from it, move forward."

"███ is a good man," she says. "But we fight. And we're both so *anxious*."

As she's talking, I feel something in my chest: a new, piercing chill. I know what it is; my hearthole is opening. I try to focus. "Everyone's anxious right now, because of the plague," I say.

Liz shakes her head and starts to weep.

"Where's ██, █?"

"I said some awful things to him, and he got very upset and—I'm so stupid, stupid!" She slaps herself in the face. "He won't answer his phone and no one has seen him. What if something happened to him?"

My chest opens wider, then wider still. "It's going to be OK."

"Nothing is OK," she weeps. "Nothing is ever going to be OK."

I think, This is my *wife*, a person I once lived with. We traveled halfway across the world together. I *loved* her, I did—her, and my poor fiancée Melody, and the Lady with the Invisible Dog. I'd once loved my mother, and my father too. And _____. And Coolidge. At times, I'd even loved *myself*. And where did that love *go*? Did it die?

If Master Elvin were here, he'd say that the love was a lie to begin with. But ██ and I had a *life* together. How could I not love my own life—every single driveway moment of it?

Suddenly I stand up, embarrassed and panicked, and I stumble through ██'s living room, out the door and across the street. My chest is cold as ice.

"Chris!" ██ says. But I don't turn back—I start speed-walking down the street. I know in my hearthole that I'm having a relapse. My brain just *thinks* I still love ██, and _____, and myself. This will pass, I tell myself—it'll pass.

But soon I'm running. Then I see red clouds in the distance; I'm not far from the west side of the colony—from the Heart-groves™. I run toward them, and within minutes my feet are splurging through the red fields. Then, in the distance, I see workers digging holes for hearts. I jump over a trench and keep moving until I am stopped in my tracks by a line of heartrees. My hearthole suddenly feels as wide as my chest.

"Hey! Unloveable!" shouts a foreman in the distance. He waves at me.

I don't respond. I stare at the tree—at the hearts hanging from the branches.

"What are you doing, Unloveable?" shouts the foreman.

Without thinking about it, I reach up and pluck a heart off the branch. I hold the heart in my hand. It's heavy. It's beating. Then I pull down the neck of my shirt and stuff the heart into my chest.

Love is real.

"Stop! Breach! Breach!" shouts the foreman.

I pull another heart down, and then another; I stuff three hearts in my chest—four hearts, five. I can feel those hearts connecting to my veins and arteries, flooding my brain with light and filling my lungs with air. Finally, I can breathe. My brain is the sea. My thoughts are the stars. My legs are pistons. I turn and run back the way I came, toward the edge of the HeartGroves™ and the city beyond. The Unloveables run after me—a whole group of them now, shouting "Freeze!" and "Stop right there, Boucher!"—but I am new and free and I know they'll never catch me.

and the moon that rejected me.

Thank you. Thank you so much for everything.

and you,

and ulcerative colitis,

I miss

and you

the trees,

and you,

and Melody

I miss everyone—everyone I've ever known.

I miss everyone—everyone I've ever known.

CHRISTOPHER BOUCHER is the author of the widely praised novels *Golden Delicious* and *How to Keep Your Volkswagen Alive*. He teaches literature and writing at Boston College, and is editor of the literary magazine *Post Road*. He lives in Northampton, Massachusetts.

Also by Christopher Boucher

• ✦ •

• ✦ •

978-1-935554-63-9

$15.00 U.S./$17.00 Can.

This title is also available as an eBook

mhpbooks.com

Also by Christopher Boucher

✦

978-1-61219-510-0

$16.95 U.S./$21.95 Can.

This title is also available as an eBook

mhpbooks.com